Undoubtedly Nishank

A Literary Reading

Undoubtedly Nishank
A Literary Reading

Gopal Sharma

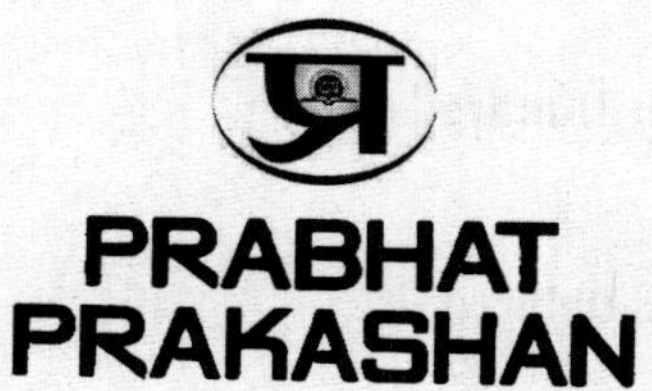

Published by
PRABHAT PRAKASHAN PVT. LTD.
4/19 Asaf Ali Road,
New Delhi-110 002 (INDIA)
e-mail: prabhatbooks@gmail.com

ISBN 978-93-90366-29-3
UNDOUBTEDLY NISHANK: A Literary Reading
by Shri Gopal Sharma

Edition
2025

Price
₹ 400.00 (Rupees Four Hundred only)

Printed at
R-Tech Offset Printers, Delhi

Foreword

I

Ramesh Pokhriyal 'Nishank' is currently India's Education Minister.[1] He is also known as 'Dr. Nishank' owing to the honorary D. Litts. that have been bestowed on him. 'Nishank,' his *nom de plume* or pen-name, featuring in the title of the present book, has been translated into English by its author, Gopal Sharma, as 'undoubtedly'. Reportedly conferred on him by the Uttarakhand writer, Nand Kishore Dhaundiyal, 'Nishank' also means confident, determined, sure, positive, convinced, unshaken, assured, unwavering—qualities that certainly apply to the subject of this book.

Born on 15 July, 1959 at Pinani, a remote village in Pauri district of Uttarakhand, Nishank's beginnings, as a horticulture worker's (*mali*) son, were humble. He started his professional life as a school teacher in Saraswati Shishu Mandir. About those days of hardship and struggle, he reminisces:

> *"I started my career as a school teacher. I saw many phases in life in which I felt that going ahead was impossible. But instead of just putting my hands on my cheeks, I put in my heart and soul to doing even the most impossible of the tasks. It is also a fact that many times, my faith in hard work wavered and on many occasions,*

1. Indeed, as Director of Indian Institute of Advanced Study, Shimla, I must offer a disclaimer at the very outset that he is my minister too. Needless to say, the views expressed in this Foreword are not related to my official position but are personal.

I thought, 'Is fate supreme?' if that is so, then why did Lord Krishna declare karma as being most superior in the Gita? If that's so, then why did Lord Rama dare to cross a vast ocean when he did not have any competent army, opportunities or weapons like those of Ravana? It's clear that only great toil contributes towards every great success."

Trust Hard Work Not Destiny
(New Delhi: Diamond Prakashan, 2013, p. v)

Undoubtedly, Nishank's relentless strivings paid off. In 1987, he was appointed the central spokesperson of the Uttaranchal (later Uttarakhand) Rajya Sangharsh Samiti, which fought for separate statehood of Uttarakhand. From 1991 to 2012, he was elected five consecutive times to the Legislative Assembly, first of India's largest state Uttar Pradesh (UP) and then of Uttarakhand, after its formation in 2000. Since 1996, after serving as a Cabinet Minister in UP, then Uttarakhand, Nishank was appointed as the fifth Chief Minister of the latter state from June 2009 to September 2011. After moving to national politics, he was twice elected to the Lok Sabha from the prestigious Haridwar constituency. Today, Nishank has risen to one of the highest cabinet positions in the country.

No wonder, most well-informed Indians are aware of his place in India's political establishment, even if they don't know the details of his tussle to the top. But, perhaps, very few know that Dr. Nishank is also an important author, with over 75 books to his credit. These include volumes of poems, short stories, novels, travelogues, biography, history and inspirational writing. His vast and growing oeuvre, mostly in Hindi, but lately in English too, is worth exploring at some length. That is precisely what Dr. Gopal Sharma, a professor of English in the Department of English Language and Literature ((DELL), Arba Minch University, Ethiopia (Africa), sets out to do in this slender volume.

Apart from its content and approach to the subject, what makes Sharma's book special is that it is the first full-length volume on 'Nishank' in English:

> *"I am addressing mainly those readers who operate in English but are largely unaware of another India around them. I am also addressing you who are going to read about him in original after scanning through this very brief introduction."*

What is more, he adds words with which Hindi parochialists may take offence, but does so very cleverly, often quoting Hindi's greatest contemporary writer of our time, Premchand.

> I prefer English because it is English that is a more powerful language than Hindi. The power of English elite has been remarkable. None other than Premchand wrote the following lines, from which we can gauge for ourselves why this language is still considered the language of the privileged.

> पुराने समय में आर्य और अनार्य का भेद था, आज अंग्रेजीदाँ और गैर-अंग्रेजीदाँ का भेद है।

In other words, while in olden times a distinction was made between *Aryas* and non-*Aryas* (the noble vs. the ignoble); today the division is between those who know English and those who don't. Whether we agree with Premchand's views in today's context or not, it is a fact that by bringing Nishank's work to the knowledge of English readers worldwide, Sharma has done a service both to his subject and to literature.

Describing him as a 'poet-cum-politician', Sharma admits that Nishank is no Premchand or Nirala, yet over 15 theses and research works have been completed on his writings. His books have been translated into many Indian and foreign languages, in addition, of course, to English. I would like to assure Sharma that his subject is certainly worthy of an in-depth study—there is no call to be defensive or anxious on this score. As Sharma quotes Shamsher Bahadur Singh, "बात बोलेगी, हम नहीं"—Nishank's work, too, will speak for itself and posterity will decide on its enduring value.

II

How does Gopal Sharma approach his subject? Let us turn to his own words to describe his literary and critical effort:

> *"The 'text' called 'Nishank' or Nishank's text is the subject of this book... I am not presenting a 'key' or 'guide' to the well-versed 'Nishank' reader. This text is a 'supplement' to the text called 'Nishank' and is undoubtedly on and about 'Nishank' the text and not 'Nishank' the 'man'."*

In other words, his book is as much about the textualisation of 'Nishank' as it is about Nishank's texts. As to the latter, Sharma does an able job indeed, devoting separate chapters to Nishank's poems, short stories, novels, as well as to other genres. He also takes up issues such as what makes Nishank write and whether he is really a great or important writer. In addition, Sharma visits and revisits notions of literariness and literary merit, realism and reality, poetics and politics, nation and narration, and, inspired by Dr. 'Arun', the values that inform Nishank's writings. Of these, humanity and humility stand out. Nishank is a writer who inspires the common reader with positive thoughts and constructive views. He is neither a practitioner of *pragativaad* (progressivism) nor *prayogvaad* (experimentation), neither an activist nor a member of any literary *avant garde,* neither a jilted lover nor an inveterate romantic.

One crucial and useful way to discover Nishank's writing is to place him in the tradition of poetic nationalism and patriotism. Citing the work of Francesca Orsini on *The Hindi Public Sphere* (2006), Sharma likens Nishank's works to that of eminent writer-politicians like Madan Mohan Malaviya and Purushottam Das Tandon, who 'established Hindi as a legitimate language of political exchange and the language of *swarajya*. Nishank's famous lines come to the mind:

सैकड़ों मस्तक चढ़े माँ, मैं भी उनमें एक हूँ।
चाहता हूँ वंदनीय माँ, क्षण व कण प्रत्येक दूँ॥

(Thousands of decapitated heads were offered to you

O Mother, I too wish to offer every mite and moment to you.)

Or

अब कोई सपना मत देखो कि भूमि बाँट ली जाएगी।
अब जो देश बाँटने की माँग करेगा, उसकी जीभ काट दी जाएगी॥

(Now don't dream of ever dividing this land
Whoever tries to split our nation, his tongue itself will be cut.)

In this context, it is vital to recall the close connection, personal, poetic and political between Nishank and the late Atal Bihari Vajpayee, who was himself a noted poet, writer, and eloquent orator. At the book-release function of one of Nishank's books, Vajpayee said:

सक्रिय राजनीति में रहते हुए भी जिस प्रखरता से डॉ. निशंक साहित्य के क्षेत्र में लगातार संघर्षरत हैं। यह आम आदमी के बस की बात नहीं है। मुझे डॉ. निशंक की संघर्षशीलता और दृढ़ इच्छा-शक्ति पर पूर्ण विश्वास है कि वे अपने राजनैतिक जीवन की व्यस्तताओं के उपरांत भी अपनी लेखनी के माध्यम से आम जनमानस की भावनाओं को उभारकर समाज और देश के सामने ऐसे प्रश्न खड़े करते रहेंगे, जिनके उत्तर के लिए कभी-न-कभी जिम्मेदार व्यक्तियों को अपने कर्तव्यों का एहसास जरूर हो जाएगा।

(Despite being in active politics, the vigour with which Dr. Nishank is constantly struggling and creating new space for himself in the realm of literature can't be attained by an ordinary man. I have full faith in the struggle and strong will-power of Dr. Nishank that he will continue to raise such questions and issues before our society and country through his writings so that the reactions and sentiments of the masses are made known to the people who are responsible for mitigating their woes also realise their duties towards them.)

As this generous encomium from Vajpayee shows, no matter how engrossed or occupied he is in politics, Nishank remains a writer, true to his art and craft.

Politics and poetics, as Nishank shows too well in *Sangharsh Jari Hai,* are identical things. The word is sacred and has its own salience. It cannot be subdued or subordinated to politics or propaganda. 'शब्द कभी मरते नहीं हैं' as Nishank himself puts it, "Words never die." The poet recognises himself only in the field of poetry: 'स्वयं को जाना है मैंने/गीत में'—(I have known myself/in my songs.) Words are Nishank's eternal friends: "यह शब्द रचना नहीं/मेरा चिर मीत है। मेरा अस्तित्व है।" His poems are not mere word-play or penmanship; they are his forever friends, his very existence. In the hurly-burly and rough-and-tumble of politics, he sometimes feels like an Abhimanyu in their *chakravyuh* or snare: दुष्प्रचार की आँधी में भी निशंक अकेला खड़ा हुआ हूँ। (Nishank stands alone in the storm of false narratives and puffery.) No wonder Vajpayee exhorted Nishank, "You can stop at anything but never stop writing."

In consonance with another of his role models, former President of India, Dr. A.P.J. Abdul Kalam, Nishank is also a writer of inspirational poems and prose. Never a pessimist, he encourages and inspires readers, especially the youth, to take up cudgels against challenges and difficulties. Dr. Yogendra Nath Sharma 'Arun' has just released a book on this genre of his writings, titled, *Dr. Nishank ka Prernatmak Chintan* (2020) ('The Inspirational Reflections of Dr. Nishank'. Like President Kalam, Nishank exhorts the youth not to be afraid ever, even of death:

भीगा हुआ आदमी कभी
बारिश से नहीं डरता,
कफन सिर पर बाँधने वाला
कभी मौत से नहीं डरता।

(One already drenched
Is never afraid of rain.
One who has tied a shroud around his head
Cannot be afraid of death.) [My translation]

There is never an escape or easy way out of the turmoil and tragedy of life. One must simply accept one's lot, gird up one's loins, so to speak, and join the fight for truth, justice and humanity. This is what his poems show us.

Nishank believes, like most Indians do, that in the end, despite whatever the odds, truth triumphs (*satyameva jayate*):

झूठ की उम्र कभी
ज्यादा नहीं होती
पर कम समय में यह दुनिया घूम लेता है।
यह कितने परिवारों
मनों और विचारों का
कत्ल कर देता है।
सच कभी हारता नहीं
इसे आने में
वक्त लगता है
लेकिन झूठ की
सभी खाइयों को
एक साथ पाटकर
भरता है।

(The untruth lifespan of untruth
Is never large.
But in a little while it travels round the world.

It kills so many families,
Minds and thoughts.
Truth is never defeated.
It takes a long time
To arrive. But
It spans and fills
All the fissures of untruth.) [My translation]

Nishank, thus, never gives in to depression or despair. His is a positive message for ordinary men and women.

From a more literary standpoint, we might locate or understand the texts of Nishank, as Sharma suggests, by placing them in the tradition of literary regionalism or what in Hindi literary criticism has come to be called as *aanchalikta.* Going back to the doyen of Hindi literature, Premchand, then taken to new heights by Phanishwar Nath 'Renu' in *Maila Aanchal* from which work the term itself derives, this special variety of regionalism in Hindi literature celebrates the life and culture of a well-defined and specific geo-cultural space. For Nishank, it is clearly Uttarakhand, a state he himself helped to form, separating it from Uttar Pradesh. As far as his home state is concerned, Nishank, to invoke Upendranath '*Ashk*', is really a *ghumta aina*, wandering mirror, a people's writer. His works not only portray the common ordinary men and women, mostly of his own knowing and experience, but also the flora, fauna and landscape of his beloved Uttarakhand.

Called '*Dev Bhoomi*', or the land of the gods, this beautiful, mostly hilly state in the lower Himalayas is famous for its natural beauty and its simple folk. Yet, it is considered the home of India's loftiest thoughts, scriptures and spiritual accomplishments. From the heights of the Himalayas to the plains of Haridwar, Uttarakhand is suffused with 'an energy of piety and simplicity' rarely to be found in the crowded and overpopulated large cities of India or even the teeming towns in the plains. It is this special quality that Nishank tries to capture and portray in his writings. Without stereotyping or condescension, he tries to relate with special empathy to the people of Uttarakhand.

Perhaps, the finest exposition of Nishank's life-values as a writer is offered by Dr. 'Arun' in *Kathakar Nishank ke Upanyason Mein Jeevan Mulya* (2017):

1. A symbol of strong expression of socio-cultural life values. —*Beera*
2. The mirror of expression of national and human values. —*Major Nirala*
3. A mirror of the strong expression of life-values of Uttarakhand society. —*Pahad se Uncha*
4. A living mirror of poignant feelings and ecstatic life-values. —*Apna Paraya*
5. An expression of woman's beauty, courage, dedication and lofty values. —*Pallavi*
6. The victory over truth and justice over injustice and untruth, good over evil. —*Pratigya*
7. Swinging between the ideal and reality. —*Chuut Gaya Padav*
8. Lively witness of the value of dignity of womanhood. —*Nishant*
9. Strong expression against negativity in life. —*Krataghna*
10. Depicting the shattered life values of the society. —*Bhagonvali*

As 'Arun' puts it, "In the absence of life-values, no human being or his society can progress or develop." This sums up the main features and characteristics of Nishank's key works and contribution to the world of literature.

III

Behind every good book is a fascinating story. This all authors, regardless of their mode of writing or the extent of their success, will probably confirm. There is a mystery about words, about their origin and destination that defies our full comprehension. No wonder, all ancient societies considered the word sacred. *Sabda*—Brahman, as the primal Hindus called it, or the cosmic word, the transcendental sound, the *mantra* of the ultimate reality, the creator of worlds, the bliss-giver and the liberator. Thus poets the world over have a secret bond, irrespective of their nation, religion, or community, provided their devotion to the word is unsullied.

That is how Dr. Sharma came to write this book and which will make an intriguing story in its own right. How I myself was invited to write this Foreword would be part of that story. There are two connecting factors. First and foremost, Dr. Yogendra Nath Sharma 'Arun', whom even the minister addresses as 'Guruji', is an eminent Hindi professor, writer, poet and litterateur. It was he who inspired Dr. Sharma to undertake this task during his spare time and, once the draft manuscript was completed, asked the author to send it to me. The other connecting factor is the holy city of Haridwar, which is not only Dr. Nishank's constituency, but also the place where Guruji served for long years as principal of an important college. Dr. Gopal Sharma also began his career in Haridwar, by the banks of River Ganga. My own Haridwar connection is Swami Rama, my guru, who has a tiny *ashram*, 'Ram Kunj', right on the riverbank. The roar of the river at night, during the magical days that I spent in the *ashram*, seemed to proclaim, '*Jai Gange, Hara Hara Gange.*' The unique Omkareshwar temple in the *ashram*, where Swami Rama himself installed the Shivalinga, seemed to hum, '*Ananda Om Hari Om*'. Given this strong uniting influence—or should I say confluence—I found myself readily agreeing to write this Foreword, the 'only connect', to quote E.M. Forster from his *Howard's End.* That is the purpose of literature, which in the Sanskrit word *sahitya,* itself means 'collective welfare'.

At the conclusion of our felicitous connection, I must say that Sharma has written both a uniquely inventive and original book. As he said to me in an e-mail:

> "You have rightly noticed that the book is less about 'Nishank' than about the author's own views on literature, criticism, poetics, translation, language, and so on. ... Let me put it in this way. This is a new kind of text. It offers new ways of thinking about literature and about reading a text critically. It is written for the readers of English and English readers who have never read a Hindi book but have a thorough background of English literary criticism and theory."

In congratulating Sharma and his effort to 'translate' Nishank, the man and the text, into English for a world-wide audience, I am reminded of George Steiner's observation in *After Babel* (1976): "The translator invades, extracts, and brings home..." This feat Sharma has certainly accomplished, reanimating, as Walter Benjamin proposes, an afterlife for Nishank's works that is even more powerful than their original life. As Sharma says so movingly, "For me, reading Nishank has been an act of replicating myself and I wish my readers too to replicate themselves when they read him."

—Makarand R. Paranjape

Director, Indian Institute of Advanced Study, Shimla

Preface

In which language do the Indian writers communicate their experiences and creative impulses? Many believe it is in English. The very first sentence of David Graddol's book '*English Next: India*' (2010) is: '*India speaks English; at least that is what most of the world imagines.*' When we say it is Hindi, the usual sceptical Western retort has been: '*Then show us in English translation.*' For instance, when Salman Rushdie edits *The Vintage Book of Indian Writing 1947-1997*, the anthology has only one writer whose original work is in an Indian language (Urdu). Sahitya Akademi and Bharatiya Jnanpith, both have been acknowledging the salutary contributions of great writers from all the prominent Indian languages, including English but somehow the English intelligentsia and readers ignore the contribution of others. To mitigate this situation, we have to very often make concentrated efforts to familiarise the readers of English and English readers with the good and great writings in other languages, including Hindi.

The name Dr. Ramesh Pokhriyal 'Nishank' needs no introduction. Do you know that he is a man of letters too? He has been writing for a very long time and the world of Hindi has been reading his poems, short stories and novels and diligently writing on and about his works. Some of his books are available in translation too. The sheer volume of his work is impressive.

The 'text' called 'Nishank' or Nishank's text is the subject of this book. I got an opportunity to read him through and through and was so impressed with the range and depth of his work that I decided to share my joy with you. The book is arranged in the manner of 'a brief introduction' and a conscious attempt has also been made to place Dr. Nishank's contribution to Hindi literature, in particular and literature in general, into consideration.

I would like to take this opportunity to thank the following for their support: Dr. Yogendra Nath Sharma 'Arun' for inspiration; Dr. Bechain Kandiyal for providing me a set of Dr. Nishank's books, Dr. Rishabha Deo Sharma for his local guardianship at Hyderabad, and last but not least, Prof. Makarand R. Paranjape for writing the Foreword.

—Gopal Sharma

Contents

1
The Pretext of the Text

हिरण्मयेनपात्रेणसत्यस्यापिहितंमुखम्।
तत्त्वंपूषन्नपावृणुसत्यधर्मायदृष्टये॥[1]

(Truth lies concealed by the golden vessel; Do thou O Sun! Open the lid so as the Truth so concealed be visible to us.)?

The Sacred Bare Truth

At the outset, let me thank you and thank you profusely as you embark on a journey with me to go through the literary output of Dr. Ramesh Pokhriyal 'Nishank'. "Who is 'Nishank'? you might ask." I had better recollect the opening line of Francis Bacon's essay '*Of Truth*', wherein he says that Pilate 'would not stay for an answer'.[2] The answer lies in the question itself. In his essay *On Truth and Lie in an Extra-Moral Sense* (1873), Nietzsche asks, 'What, then, is truth?' And proposes a reply, "Truths are illusions about which one has forgotten that this is what they are."[3] In *Truth and Method,* Gadamer says that understanding is always a matter of interpretation and it can be understood by language. The truth is always hidden. The seeker should better find the truth for himself. How should you and I seek it? Read. 'Read' (*Iqra)* is the first word of the Holy Quran, brought down upon the Holy Prophet (PBUH) by Allah in the caves of Hira.

But beware! Don't be impatient. '*Sabr*' is another word in Arabic. It means patience. If you come face to face with truth, you will understand what I mean. You needn't go on a pilgrimage to *Koh-e-Toor* to get revelation. The Truth has always been present in poetry and literature.

आम है यार की तज्जली 'मीर'।
खास मूसा-ए-कोहे-तूर नहीं।।[4]

His effulgence is everywhere; not confined to Moses and the Mount of Sinai. On the mountain of Sinai, God is supposed to have revealed Himself to Moses who was so dazzled by the light as to become unconscious. The Truth dazzles and can make the viewer blind. That is why, as the American poetess Emily Dickinson says, "Truth must dazzle gradually or every person will be blind."

Tell all the Truth but tell it slant –
Success in circuit lies
too bright for our infirm delight.
The Truth's superb surprise.[5]

Dickinson says that we should tell the truth—the entire truth—but tell it indirectly, in a circuitous and round-the-houses manner. The truth is too bright and dazzling for us to be able to cope with it in one attempt. We can get overwhelmed by it. Therefore, we will read 'Nishank' slowly but steadily to know and realise the truth about his work. I will eschew Stendhal Syndrome in response to the immense beauty present here and there. The truth for which the author Nishank stands for and the values his text enshrines in are worth observing. We will also follow the advice given by the poetess as we know that literature is nothing but the truth embalmed with delicious icing. The 'truth's superb surprise' will be gained by you and I, only if we very patiently read him as a text. I am going to read him closely and find out the truth. And for your education and delight, I will tell it slant.

कबित बिबेक एक नहीं मोरे।
सत्य कहहूँ लिखी कागद कोरे।।

—*तुलसीदास*

(I have got no poetic and creative excellence; I merely speak truth by writing on blank sheets of paper.)

This has been a submissive and gentle stance of the great poets ranging from Kalidas to Tulsidas in India. But I can't say that I have neither experience nor the talent to write a book. I do have the knack of writing such books as this. There is a secret and I am not going to reveal it.

At the outset, I am being religious and invoking scriptures. In fact, Truth and God are same and have as much to do with the practice of literary criticism as with the nature of literature. What German philosopher Adorno says about art is 'Magic delivered from the lie of being truth' it is true to literature and life too. For me and several other Indians of my age, a poet is akin to Brahma and 'a poem is the very image of life expressed in its eternal truth' (Shelley). Literature is as sacred as religion and literature can be a form of religion for the secular mindset. Salman Rushdie also describes literature as a sanctuary, saying it is "the one place in any society where, within the secrecy of our own heads, we can hear the voices talking about everything in every possible way."[6] This text, then, is a sacred text. And I am a twice-born Pundit! (*pun intended*).

Profiling Dr. Ramesh Pokhriyal 'Nishank'

> *"I love this name (Derrida), which is not mine, of course. The only possibility of loving a name is that it is not yours."*[7]
>
> *—Derrida*

There is a visible connection between a name and an entire oeuvre. The name, Nishank, has potency about it. The name is a kind of shorthand designation for his entire literary achievement and his public persona. We have Nirala, Nagarjuna, Dhumil and Dinkar; we know pretty well what we mean when we say that Agyeya is a poet whose life is recorded across the entire body of his work. In the same way, I know what I mean when I say 'Nishank'.

Dr. Ramesh Pokhriyal 'Nishank' is a multi-faceted personality who experiences the topsy-turvy reality of politics and the mutant of literature, representing both in his own wonderful style. For him politics and literature have been the means of rejuvenating our society, its morals, ideals, religion and culture. Most of his work is stepped in national consciousness, social concerns and a rabid sense of humanism and universalism. As a judicious politician and devoted social worker, his persona is of a common man attached to his motherland and one who never forgets his roots and difficult phases of his early life spent in the Uttarakhand region.

Ramesh was not born with a silver spoon in his mouth. His father was an employee in the horticulture department and the boy Ramesh lived an ordinary early life along with his family. His life was flat, level and plain where he faced a number of road-blocks. His formative days were far from the maddening metro-crowd. He was never adrift from the toiling masses. No one can escape the vicissitudes of life. His life too was not a bed of roses. In one of his self-help books, he writes.

> *"I started my career as a school teacher. I saw many phases in life in which I felt that going ahead was impossible. But instead of just putting my hands on my cheeks, I gave my heart and soul to do even the impossible tasks. It is also a fact that many times, my faith in hard work shook and on many occasions, I thought, 'Is fate supreme?' if that is so, then why did Lord Krishna declare karma as the most superior in the Gita? If that's so, then why did Lord Rama dared to cross a vast ocean when he did not have a competent army, opportunities and weapons vis-a-vis those of Ravana? It's clear that only great toil contributes towards every great success."*[8]

Yes, now that Dr. Nishank is not an ordinary face in the crowd and is a personality that matters, it is easy to praise him and his village and surroundings. I should resist the temptation of presenting here some truths about his life from birth till now. At present, it is repeatedly said that he hails from Pinani village in Pauri, a district which has produced personalities like Uttar Pradesh Chief Minister Yogi Adityanath, Uttarakhand Chief Minister Trivendra Singh Rawat, Army Chief Bipin Rawat and National Security Adviser Ajit Doval. He was born in the state from where Sumitra Nandan Pant and Gaura Pant 'Shivani' arrived and made a mark in the world of literature. But it doesn't mean much as there must have been so many others who didn't get an opportunity to come up well in life. I was born in the same town where Vishnu Prabhakar was born, but the comparison stops there. Still, we shouldn't 'let ambition mock their useful toil' who, like many of us, couldn't make a mark.

> Full many a gem of purest ray serene,
> The dark unfathom'd caves of ocean bear:
> Full many a flow'r is born to blush unseen,
> And waste its sweetness on the desert air.[9]

Thank God, Dr. Nishank didn't remain 'a mute inglorious Milton' and kept the 'noiseless tenor' speak for itself when his time came. That is why we can proudly say that by his writing, Hindi has been enriched and Hindi speakers have been enabled to hold their heads high in the world. When I show any of Nishank's books to a stranger (someone from another language and country) it is as if I ask him with gentle pride, 'Have you anyone to match this? Is your Education Minister also like ours?' Dr. Ramesh Pokhriyal 'Nishank' sits in the chair where Moulana Abul Kalam Azad, K.L. Shrimali, Humayun Kabir, M.C. Chagla, Atal Bihari Vajpayee and Murli Manohar Joshi sat. He has the task of changing the very course of our education system. His erudite scholarship and literary sensibility is going to help him see through the scandalous ways of some of the faculty and students.

A journalist-turned-politician, who started his career as a teacher in Saraswati Sishu Mandir and went on to become the Education Minister, is a wonder of our democracy in which talent couldn't go unnoticed. It is not just a matter of date but his date of birth is 15th of August, 1959. It indicated in its own mysterious ways that he was born to charm the people with his yeoman service to the nation. I don't know if he has telepathic powers like Salman Rushdie's *Midnight's Children* but I am sure about Dr. Nishank that he is a man befitting his name. As a man of letters, Dr. Nishank has authored more than 75 books which include novels, short stories, selection of poems, biographies, travelogues, etc. As a political person, he has been an MLA, Chief Minister, state minister and M.P. etc.; presently, he is a Lok Sabha M.P. and is a cabinet minister serving as Education Minister in the second Narendra Modi ministry. He represents Haridwar Parliamentary constituency of Uttarakhand in the 17th Lok Sabha. But please hang on...

If you really wanted to know where he was born and what his childhood was like and how his parents were occupied and all the details before he became the talk of the town, and all that unnecessary and unrelated biographical crap, go and directly ask him. Better Google his name or go to his official website.

We are not here to read about one who happens to be a politician and a minister. His literary pursuit is our immediate concern. He is here around me in the form of his books. I can see his photograph on almost all the books he wrote but those photographs are simply a fraction of a wide open text.

British critics I.A. Richards and F.R. Leavis involved a way of reading that emphasised form—the importance of considering 'the words on the page'—rather than factors, such as the life of the author and his or her intentions, or the historical and ideological context in which the text was produced. After all, what is in a name? I don't know the individual Nishank. His full name and surname, family details and designation are not required as such. These matter little to me. I understand the meaning of the dictum 'familiarity breeds contempt' very well. Once Hegel said, "What is familiarly known is not properly known, just for the reason that it is familiar."[10] Therefore, let us not bother about his details too much. It doesn't mean that there is no value of the authorial voice in the text. He fathered his texts. When we, as readers or listeners, are reading those texts, there is somewhere its author seated in comfort or commotion. No one can and no one should ignore the author completely. Dr. Nishank has been writing as a solitary sentinel to protect our solidarity and nationhood. He has no time to revise what he writes. Instead, he has an insatiable desire to express himself in words. Whenever he gets time, he writes. He doesn't stand and wait so that the damsel of learning or Devi Saraswati comes and blesses him. He is a reader impatient to read what he has felt so abidingly. That is why my admiration for a reader-writer or the readers' writer is paramount.

Why have I chosen to write a book on him and not any other well-known and well-placed person? What is so great about him? 'Why Nishank?' you might ask. And my retort is, 'Why not?' This is the book I decided to write in my own way and style. The decision didn't change the fact that I have neither a stance nor attitude. I have a singular aim, undecided and undefiled.

Keeping the usual retort and repartee aside, let me admit that I got the entire set of books written by Dr. Nishank in PDF form as well and I have been reading these without any break. The Corona days didn't let anyone go outside and I too followed WHO norms of 'social distancing'. ('It was the best of times; it was the worst of times,' to quote Charles Dickens). Reading, contemplating and writing went on in an orderly fashion, not necessarily in the given order. One who has been given the task of overhauling, formulating and transforming the entire gamut of our education system, must be a noble soul and an accomplished author, I envisaged. And the 'rest is history'.

Nishank as a Text

'With the word with; them, begins this text whose first line tells the truth.'[11] Francis Ponge (1899-1988), French essayist and poet said this to underline the value of a text as truth.

In a truly liberated Foucaldian sense, I shall honour the text over the author. In 1967, Roland Barthes, the eminent French theorist, in his highly influential essay *Death of the Author* tried to underline the value of a text and placed it above the author. We will also read the text through and through. For me Nishank is the name of a text. The text will reveal the truth as the truth lies in the text. Algerian-born French philosopher Jacques Derrida said, 'There is nothing outside the text' (*il n'y a pas d'hors-texte*). When Derrida first formulated this thought in his book, *On Grammatology*, he meant that the meaning of the text must be situated within a context of the text.

The bulk of Nishank's text, his entire oeuvre, will astound anyone as he has been a prolific writer. No matter, as the text is always open. We can enter from any side and can exit any time as and when we feel inconvenient. There are only ten doors in human anatomy but a framework created by a writer is as broad as daylight and as wide as the cosmos. A door is an entrance and exit at the same time.

This book is also a text. It is the text prepared by reading the text called Nishank. Does Nishank's text belong to him? No, I think that he writes, as George Bernard Shaw said, for the same reason as the cow gives milk: it's inside him. It's got to come out and in a real sense, he would suffer if he couldn't. It's the way he expresses his reaction to the world he lives in, sees around him and tries to imagine. It would be as futile to claim ownership of the milk for a cow to assert that she owns the milk she has provided. No, the text no longer belongs to the writer; it belongs to you, the reader.

I repeat what I learnt by reading Derrida. Derrida made it clear that the text has no stable identity, no stable origin and no stable end. Each act of reading the text is a preface to the next. Once William Blake wrote, "I must create a system or be enslaved by another man's."[12] Am I going to read Nishank keeping in view all the unsolicited suggestions offered to me? There are scholars who say that the best way to go to a writer is to find out various discourses, universal human values, prevalent isms, etc. Matthew Arnold proposed the 'touchstone method' of evaluation as a corrective for what he called the 'fallacious' estimates of poems according to their 'historic' importance in the development of literature, or else according to their 'personal' appeal to an individual critic. I listened to all the suggestions offered to me but there was in me my guide, William Shakespeare, who told me otherwise. He said to me, "Do as you like?" In one of the Shakespeare's play *As You Like It*, there is a character named Touchstone. He is a wise fool who acts as a kind of guide to others. I don't want to turn into a wise fool. I also don't want to be Robert Frost's narrator who habitually wastes his energy in regretting any choice that is made. There are persons who regret no matter which road they go. They will be sorry that they didn't go the other way.

> Two roads diverged in a wood and
> I took the one less travelled by
> And that has made all the difference.[13]

To understand a part, you must understand the whole in which it resides; but to understand the whole, you must understand the individual part that makes up the whole. It is the standard hermeneutic paradox. As I am familiar with this paradox and have been a student of Derrida, I will keep in mind both. My sojourn along with you is directed towards no goal. I will have no regrets of any kind. Emerson says, 'Life is a journey and not the destination.' The real pleasure in life is in the journey. As Bennington rightly says, 'Deconstruction happens more in the journey than the arrival.'[14] When I will see these words printed in the form of a book, I shall get the feeling of a work accomplished. That moment will be transitory and transient.

When I write these lines, the pleasure I am getting is beyond words. Read these lines, between the lines and beyond the lines—you too will share my joy and pleasure. Was it a vision or a waking dream? If my writing is a joyful experience, your reading-response will also follow suit. My reading and interpretation, to borrow Norman Holland's words, is according to my identity; your reading is according to yours as 'all of us, as we read, use the literary work to symbolise and finally to replicate ourselves.'[15] That is why my reading is less 'faithful' and more 'individual'. I approach Nishank through his published work rather than through scanty and cursory critical appraisals based on a thematic study of his work. For me the author is already separated from his work and I needn't invoke him to understand the text. But when I wish to 'give a text an author' (Barthes), I will do so wholeheartedly. In addition to this job, as a critic, I shall do what T.S. Eliot enumerates, in the introduction to *The Sacred Wood,* the duties of the critic.

> *"It is part of the business of the critic to preserve tradition where a good tradition exists. It is part of his business to see literature steadily and to see it whole; and this is eminently to see it not as consecrated by time, but to see it beyond time; to see the best work of our time and the best work of twenty-five hundred years ago with the same eyes."*[16]

The kind of close reading for which Eliot was arguing in 1919 remains the foundation of literary criticism in 2019-2020 also. I wish to perform my duty accordingly.

People say that the present is perpetual, though it is also fleeing very fast. The past and the future are nothing but the slaves and followers of the present. In the conclusion to *The Renaissance,* Walter Pater puts this concisely when he describes the present moment as 'gone while we try to apprehend it'. The Nishank text is written in the present but when it reaches the reader, it is already past and only future will tell its worth. I acknowledge and accept that in the Hindi language, the word कल can be used intermittently and interchangeably for past and future, both. If we recall, our Sanskrit literature is replete with examples in which the word 'is' (अस्ति) has been used in the beginning of stories and even epics. For instance, in the epic *Kumarsambhavam* Kavikulguru Kalidas starts with the word *astyuttarasyam* which clearly states that 'present' is the time we should always think of first. I have cited, recited, analysed and liked the discussion about time. Longevity in literature and life, both belong to the realm of destiny.

Hindi and English

Critics have different opinions about the advent of the Englishmen and the English language in India. When *khadi boli* (the standard language) was replacing Braj *bhasha* (the so-called vernacular) and other languages and was taking shape as Hindi, English too was trying to replace languages of the court, namely Arabic and Persian. We have learnt the art of balancing two languages now. Hindi and English, both have a constitutional obligation. Rashmi Sadana in *English Heart, Hindi Heartland* (2012) examines the post-colonial Indian literary world and finds that English does not represent a fixed pole in Hindi heartland but a different kind of 'literary nationality' is being perceived there. Literary translations are not a rarity now. Once Salman Rushdie said that an Indian writer expresses his multiform experiences best in English and that 'Indian Writing in English (IWE)' is simply stronger and more important than the writing in Indian vernaculars. His conclusion was based on his scanty reading. He couldn't read because the best of Indian literature was not available to him in translation. The lack of first-rate translation and the discussion of our languages through English were two significant reasons for this handicap. The Nobel laureate V.S. Naipaul wrote in *An Area of Darkness* that "What I read of them, didn't encourage me to read more. Premchand turned out to be a minor fabulist."[17] Naipaul wrote this in 1964, when there was hardly any significant translation activity in India.

Gone are the days when even Premchand's grandson Alok Rai said that Hindi was a bit of a lost cause; India of 21st century is different. On the literary map of the world, only Sanskrit literature from India used to get the place of pride. Hindi was far behind. But slowly and surely, the time is in fast forward mode now. The reach of Hindi is widespread and where its reach is disturbed, it changes its garb. Hindi becomes Hinglish. The wedding and welding of two strong languages of the world is exemplary. The hostility between Hindi and English is just for namesake or to show-off; it is not real. Scholars say that between Hindi and English, a sort of linguistic love-hate relationship has grown which has resulted in the Englishisation of Hindi and the Indianisation of English. Ram Manohar Lohia and others were hell-bent to exterminate English but to no avail. They continued their struggle for a long time and English, with the backing of the constitution and leaders, such as Nehru, remained well-placed. Article 343 of the Indian Constitution, point 1, specifically mentions, 'The official language of the Union shall be Hindi in Devanagari script. The form of numerals to be used for the official purposes of the Union shall be the international form of Indian numerals.' English is used for official purposes, such as in parliamentary proceedings, judiciary, communications between the Central Government and a state governments. States within India have the liberty and powers to specify their own official language(s) through legislation. In addition to the official languages, the Constitution recognises 22 regional languages, which include Hindi but not English, as scheduled languages. Realising all this, just the other day, Raghuvir Sahay wrote a couplet in Hindi on English. His tongue-in-cheek remark is pungent, but true:

अंग्रेजों ने अंग्रेजी पढ़ाकर प्रजा बनाई।
अंग्रेजी पढ़ाकर अब हम प्रजा बना रहे हैं॥[18]

(The English taught us English to turn us into subjects
Now we teach English to Bullying subjects.)

Now is the time of Hindi. Modi speaks Hindi; Amit Shah speaks Hindi. What was anticipated by Sudama Pandey 'Dhumil' once in his poem *Bhasha ki Raat* in the context of the language agitation of the 1960s, no longer holds true. When Prime Minister speaks in multiple languages at 'Howdy

Modi', he sets the tone and tenor of our language policy. When Bharatiya Jnanpith bestows its highest award on a novelist named Amitav Ghosh, who writes in English, we acknowledge something great. Hindi and English are two sides of the same coin. Harish Trivedi concludes his essay *Progress of Hindi* with the words, "Both Hindi and English inhabiting (while also contesting with apparent civility) the domestic space of the Indian nation, with Hindi perhaps as the fading *jethani* and the younger English as the more indulgent *devrani*." I use his forecast and wish to cast it in a new lingo.

Why English?

Yeats said, "No man can think or write with music and vigour except in his mother tongue." It is natural that Nishank writes in his mother tongue. He has also demolished the myth perpetuated by the previous ministers and politicians. *Paanch saal raaj karte hain angrezi mein, aur phir aake vote maangte hain Hindi mein!* (They rule over us for five years in English, and then they come and plead for votes in Hindi!) Nishank is a poet-politician who uses Hindi as he is expected to; 'no more, nor less' (*King Lear*). His literary output is mostly in Hindi.

But this book is not a novel, short story or a selection of poems. It isn't a piece of creative writing in the strict sense of the term. I am a fit example of Max Hawthorne's dictum, 'Those who can write, write, and those who can't criticise.' I am addressing mainly those readers who operate in English and are largely unaware of another India around them. I am also addressing you who is going to read him in original after scanning through this very brief introduction. I am also following what Acharya Mahavir Prasad Dwivedi requested in September 1914 (*see Sarswati* magazine: *Hindustaniyon ke angrezi lekh*) to do. He wanted us to use Hindi and English, both to spread the message of Hindi among all and sundry.

This book was written in English because I had a reader like you in mind. You may ask another question 'Why English?' Why do I write a text in English when the author is a Hindi litterateur? I would like to say that I chose this language (English) and not that language (Hindi) as the medium of expression just to reach a broader audience. Notwithstanding my national pride and love for my mother tongue, I prefer English because it is English that is a more powerful language than Hindi. The power of English elite has been remarkable. None other than Premchand wrote the following lines and we can see for ourselves that this language is still the language of privilege.

पुराने समय में आर्य और अनार्य का भेद था,
आज अंग्रेजीदाँ और गैर-अंग्रेजीदाँ का भेद है।[19]

> (In olden times, there was discrimination between the Aryan and the non-Aryan, today it exists between those who know English and those who don't.)

In an essay very aptly called *The Caste of English* (1978), the novelist Raja Rao underlined the oppressive nature of traditional Indian society in suppressing linguistic polyphony and polysemy and led him to attribute a caste (*varna*) to the English language by placing it on the same elevated pedestal of Truth as accorded by Brahmins only to Sanskrit. Rao accepts English "not as a guest or friend, but as our own, of our caste, our creed, our sect and of our tradition."

Truth, said a great Indian sage, is not the monopoly of the Sanskrit language. Truth can use any language and the more universal, the better it is! And as long as the English language in universal, it will always remain Indian.[20]

The multitude of Indians wishes to master English and if they can't, they leave no stone unturned to let their offspring learn it. Now that we are in the predominantly internet and social media age, we should rush to compete with English to assert our identity and distinctive features. There are so many Indians who are more proficient in the English language than in Hindi and it will be worthwhile to familiarise them with the works of notable writers of Hindi. This is a kind of 'reach out' effort in the realm of creative writing. What is the harm if some English readers also find the book worth reading?

Dr. Nishank's Profile[21]

Shri Ramesh Pokhriyal 'Nishank' was born in 1959 in a remote village, Pinani of Pauri district of Uttarakhand. His early childhood lacked in many aspects due to his financially humble background. Despite this, the brilliance of his intellect stood out. He initially served the society as a teacher and later as a journalist. His political journey started in 1987 as the central spokesperson of the Uttar Pradesh (now Uttarakhand) Sangharsh Samiti. In 1991, he was elected as an MLA from the Karnprayag Assembly. In 1996, for the first time, he became a Cabinet Minister in Uttar Pradesh. With the establishment of the Uttarakhand state, he became the Finance Minister and was handed over 12 important departments. In the year 2007, he became the Cabinet Minister and in 2009, the Chief Minister of the state. He was elected as a member of the sixteenth Lok Sabha of India from Haridwar with an overwhelming majority of MPs. Re-elected from this Lok Sabha in the year 2019, he has now taken up the important responsibility of the Ministry of Human Resource Development, Government of India. He is recognised in the country and abroad as a writer, litterateur, poet, sensitive thinker on the Himalayas and the Ganges. He has raised sensitive issues of the Himalayas and the Ganges in the Parliament. His contribution to Ganga cleanliness, especially by leading *Sparsh Ganga* campaign, has encouraged active public participation for the cause. About 15 people has either completed or are engaged in research on his literature. He has written more than 75 books, most of which have been translated into every Indian and different foreign languages. More than 15 countries had honoured him. Our country is constantly benefiting from such an honourable Human Resource Development minister.

(In this book, it is considered appropriate to use Nishank with the prefix, Dr., an agentive noun uniformly and without a period or full-stop as far as possible. The purpose is not to impress upon the reader his credentials etc. It is just a form of reverence. I find that in almost all books he is referred as

'Dr. Nishank'. I am also reminded by one of my friends that the readers in English and English readers, both are familiar with this kind of honorific. Samuel Johnson (1709-1784) is often referred as Dr. Johnson. Therefore, I am going to frequently use Dr. Nishank for Dr. Ramesh Pokhriyal 'Nishank'.)

□

2
Why Dr. Nishank Writes

*Millions of artists create; only a few thousands are discussed or accepted by the spectator and many less again are consecrated by posterity.** —*Marcel Duchamp*

Of course, I have imitated the title of this chapter from an essay written by George Orwell. There is no harm in using his essay on *Why I Write* (1946) as a take-off point. It is quite interesting to know why someone writes and writes continuously without a break. Once you know the answer of this question, you stumble upon the unauthorised biography of an author spread around his work. The bulk of Nishank's writing is perplexing and mesmerising. When does he get the spare time to write? Where does he write? How does he write? He is neither Chetan Bhagat nor Amitav Ghosh. He writes in the language that is associated with the masses and not the classes. The sheer volume of his work—more than 75 books so far—would place him in the company of the greatest of the great. Yet, he is neither Premchand nor Nirala.

Thank you for reminding me, friend! Yes, you are right. In a way, Dr. Ramesh Pokhriyal 'Nishank' is like them too, at least in name. His *nom de plume* (pen name) is *Nishank* (without any doubt, it is 'doubtless', literally and figuratively) as Premchand and Nirala both are pen names of Dhanpat Rai and Surya Kant Tripathi, respectively. Dr. Nand Kishore Dhondiyal gave him the pen-name 'Nishank'. When I was leafing through *Kabir*

Granthavali [(Ed.) Shyam Sundar Das] I came across the following couplet:

चेतनि चौकी बैसि करि, सत्‌गुरु दीन्हाँ धीर।
निरभै होइ निसंक भजि, केवल कहै कबीर॥[1]

Kabir was very much for being fearless and bold. Steadfastness was a virtue for Kabir and he wanted his followers to be bold and undoubtedly true. He was of the view that being without doubt is a quality worth emulating. Should we call this title a sobriquet in the case of Dr. Pokhriyal? He himself didn't invent it for his own embellishment. His full name needn't be repeated as I am more concerned with his text and it shouldn't be a mere pretext to speak volumes about him by citing his full name and designation. I can devote a separate chapter to speak volumes about him. Dr. Ramesh Pokhriyal 'Nishank' is a leading senior writer within Indian literature, in general and Hindi literature, in particular. In his novels, short stories, and poems centred on village and rural life of Uttarakhand, he combines nationalism with everyday experiences and elements of culture and tradition to explore the vicissitudes and aspirations of the Indian masses. His poetry too is the poetry of the heart-felt emotions with a nationalistic fervour. Dr. Nishank has been greatly influenced by the political and social life of post-Independence situations. His writings are not read for magic realism or ostentatious style, but are eulogised for a style that has a minimal touch of verbal combat and superficial decoration. It's straight from the heart to heart. That's why the subtle nuances of character, motivation and emotion very evocatively capture the reader's imagination.

Let me take the authoritarian liberty and write something related and interconnected with his pen-name. It is just my gut feeling that the pen-name 'Nishank' has some connection with Tagore's poem, '*Where the Mind is Without Fear*'. I fail to resist my temptation and would like you to appreciate the following lines once again, as the purpose is to put forward as a flash of lightning the value and meaning of 'Nishank' before you.

Where the mind is without fear
And the head is held high,
Where knowledge is free.
Where the world has not been broken up into fragments
By narrow domestic walls
Where words come out from the depth of truth,
Where tireless striving stretches its arms toward perfection
Where the clear stream of reason has not lost its way
Into the dreary desert sand of dead habit
Where the mind is led forward by thee
Into ever widening thought and action
In to that heaven of freedom,
My father LET MY COUNTRY AWAKE![2]

Nishank is the embodiment and incarnation of all these virtues envisaged in these poetic and prophetic lines. Therefore, an awakened soul, Nishank, is an awakened poet and author. Namvar Singh says that an 'awakened poet', during the process of his poetic act, keeps on defining the political contexts in a very cautious manner and thus, while avoiding to write directly on political issues, gives every creative piece a definite political meaning.[3] Thus, a poet at heart and politician by vocation writes as a social reformer.

And Nishank writes. He writes and is ready to answer the question very fondly asked by Gajanan Madhav Muktibodh, 'Partner! Do tell me your politics' (पार्टनर, अपनी पॉलिटिक्स तो बताओ)! His politics lies not in party-politics but seems to be deep-rooted in his abiding devotion to Bharatmata. He is a breath of fresh air in the forest of thoughtless and meaningless literary pursuits. He tells his politics and tells it straight.

मेरा उद्देश्य भावी पीढ़ी में राष्ट्रीयता की भावना कूट-कूटकर भरना एवं जन-जन को देशभक्ति से ओत-प्रोत करते हुए मातृभूमि के लिए सर्वस्व न्योछावर करने की भावना को जाग्रत करना है।[4]

> (My aim is to enlighten the spirit of nationalism in the coming generation and awaken the spirit of patriotism in them so that every single person is ready to sacrifice everything for the sake of the motherland.)

The above quoted line—a single line, tells us—that here is an author, novelist, short-story writer and politician rolled into one. This is Dr. Nishank's introductory remark in his preface to a collection of poems. He is a poet speaking as a poet-cum-politician. This is not an accident; it happens all the time. The ancient Greek origin of the word poetry is the verb *Poiein* which literally means 'to make or do it'. Politicians also do things with the words. Like the poets, like the novelists and others, politicians also make up stories and their desire to communicate and communicate well is well known. A politician and a poet, both are bound up with the democratic ideal of 'freedom of speech and expression'. In this way, literature and the political sphere have a close relationship. When Dr. Nishank writes, his poetic sensibility and political acumen combine together. That is why we find him writing for a cause. He is not writing for 'writing's sake'. He writes with a sense of higher and noble purpose of awakening the Indian people.

Before we come to the main point of this chapter and discuss it at length, we should go through what other writers, the great and famous ones, said about the obsession of writing creatively. Orwell lists 'four great motives for writing' which, he feels, exist in every writer. He explains that all are present, but in different proportions and also that these proportions vary from time to time. They are as follows:

1. *Sheer egoism:* Orwell argues that a writer writes from a 'desire to seem clever, to be talked about, to be remembered after death, to get your own back on grown-ups who snubbed you in childhood, etc.' He says that this is a motive the writer shares with scientists, artists, lawyers—'the whole top crust of humanity' and that the great mass of humanity, not

acutely selfish, after the age of about thirty abandons individual ambition. A minority remains, however, determined 'to live their own lives to the end and writers belong in this class.' Serious writers are vainer than journalists, though 'less interested in money'.

2. *Aesthetic enthusiasm:* Orwell explains that the present in writing is the desire to make one's writing look and sound good, having 'pleasure in the impact of one sound on another, in the firmness of good prose or the rhythm of a good story.' He says that this motive is 'very feeble in a lot of writers' but still present in all works of writing.
3. *Historical impulse:* He sums this up by stating that the motive is the 'desire to see things as they are, to find out true facts and store them up for the use of posterity.'
4. *Political purpose:* Orwell writes that 'no book is genuinely free from political bias', and further explains that this motive is used very commonly in all forms of writing in the broadest sense, citing a 'desire to push the world in a certain direction' in every person. He concludes by saying that 'the opinion that art should have nothing to do with politics is itself a political attitude.'[5]

Joan Didion, one of the most celebrated and distinctive voices of American fiction and literary journalism, delivered a lecture at University of California at Berkeley in 1976 and used Orwell's title '*Why I Write*'. She underlined 'I' which was used three times in the topic and said, "*In many ways writing is the act of saying 'I', of imposing oneself upon other people, of saying listen to me, see it my way, change your mind. It's an aggressive, even hostile act.*" [6] *Joan Didion* opines that there is nothing like a good writer or a bad writer; a writer is a writer. A writer is simply a writer. He/she is a person who's most absorbed and his passionate hours are spent arranging words on pieces of paper.

If one reads only some of the introductory prefaces (*apni baat*) written by Nishank, one can very well understand that he writes with a purpose. (Don't ask me if someone writes without a purpose?) This purpose is neither sheer egoism nor the other three reasons presented by Orwell. E.M. Forster, the great novelist, also admitted frankly that he wrote for two reasons: partly to make money and partly to win the respect of people whom he respected. His candid admission can be refuted by many other authors who have generally been claiming that they write for 'self-gratification' and 'self-actualisation'. I understand and understand squarely: we write mainly to be read and appreciated. Epic poets could say that they write for *swantahsukhay* (self-gratification). An average language author generally writes not for money but readership. There is little doubt that Dr. Nishank must have some of these aims in the beginning of his career. As a teacher and journalist, Dr. Nishank must have had his social responsibility angle also in view and through his writing, he was given to expressing the predicaments and aspirations of his people. The characters he portrays and the feelings he conveys are not unearthly; they are of this world. He is no *ethereal minstrel* like the *Skylark* of William Wordsworth, beating its wings in vain. He is also not like Shelley, 'a beautiful and ineffectual angel beating in the void his luminous wings in vain.' He, like Sir Walter Scott, writes with a purpose. Don't treat my comparison too far-fetched and airy. I am going to discuss this at length to validate my claim.

So far so good. Let me say that Nishank doesn't write as distinctively as Premchand as well. Premchand is very fondly addressed as '*kalam ka sipahi*' and '*kalam ka mazdoor*'. Premchand hardly wrote a story for free and charged handsomely for his novels. He switched to Hindi because he found writing in Urdu was not profitable. His motive was very similar to Forster's in this respect. But when Premchand wrote, he was also directly and indirectly writing to contribute in the freedom struggle spearheaded by Gandhiji. Premchand was Premchand and no other Hindi author can be compared with his stature. We are discussing him just to say that the purpose of literature and the purpose of writing and the author's purpose are complementary.

Dr. Ramesh Pokhriyal 'Nishank', the poet, novelist and story teller, has been writing for a long time. He has been active for long as a social worker, teacher, journalist and a political person. In addition, he has been writing self-help books and is well known as a motivational author. Though it is naïve to ask such a question, yet it is being asked purposely and repeatedly, 'why does he write?' The answer can be found somewhere in his text, I presume.

I could very well surmise when Nishank writes, he writes for inspiring his readers to nation-building and leading a virtuous life. Premchand had a social purpose; Nishank has his eyes fixed on the social upgradation and welfare as well. Both speak the language of social reformers when they write about the purpose of literature, in general and the purpose of their writing, in particular. Nishank must have also read Premchand a great many times, at least during his school and college days. It is also possible that Nishank has also taken a leaf out of Premchand's life and ideals. When one reads Nishank, one is reminded of Premchand. It seems that Nishank's voluminous work takes a leaf out of Premchand's essay, *The Nature and Purpose of Literature.* Delivering the presidential address at the First All India Progressive Writer's Conference held at Lucknow on 9-10 April, 1936, Premchand proclaimed:

> जब तक साहित्य का काम केवल मन-बहलाव का सामान जुटाना, केवल लोरियाँ गा-गाकर सुलाना, केवल आँसू बहाकर जी हलका करना था, तब तक इसके लिए कर्म की आवश्यकता न थी। वह एक दीवाना था, जिसका गम दूसरे खाते थे, मगर हम साहित्य को केवल मनोरंजन और विलासिता की वस्तु नहीं समझते। हमारी कसौटी पर वही साहित्य खरा उतरेगा, जिसमें उच्च चिंतन हो, स्वाधीनता का भाव हो, सौंदर्य का सार हो, सृजन की आत्मा हो, जीवन की सच्चाइयों का प्रकाश हो, जो हममें

> गति और बेचैनी पैदा करे, सुलाए नहीं, क्योंकि अब और ज्यादा सोना मृत्यु का लक्षण है।[7]
>
> (So long as it was a means of escape from life, when it demanded a mere shedding of tears over life and its sorrows, an active participation in the social struggles was not required from a literary man. We, however, have a different conception of literature and the duties of a writer. We shall consider only that literature as progressive which is thoughtful, which awakens in us the spirit of freedom and of beauty; which is creative; which is luminous with the realities of life; which moves us; which leads us to action and which does not set on us as a narcotic; which does not produce in us a state of intellectual somnolence for, if we continue to remain in that state it can only mean that we are no longer alive.)

Nishank sets his firm feet like Premchand when he writes a few words of introduction in his selection of stories *Tute Dayre*:

> संघर्ष और चुनौतियों से जो रिश्ता हमारे जीवन का है, वही रास्ता सार्थक साहित्य का भी है। प्रतिबद्धता की मशाल लिये निरंतर अन्याय व अँधेरे से जूझना इन दोनों का धर्म है। जीवन और साहित्य तभी सार्थक हैं, जब ये जनोन्मुखी और जनसरोकारी हों। लोकहित की भावना से अनुप्राणित हों। साहित्य की भी इसीलिए कलागत उपयोगिता ज्यादा है। यह हमारी सभ्यता, संस्कृति की पहचान ही नहीं, जीवन-मूल्यों की धड़कन भी है।[8]
>
> (The relationship related to our life with struggle and challenges is also related to meaningful literature. Burning the torch of commitment, battling with constant injustice and darkness is their religion. Life and literature are meaningful only when they are people oriented and public oriented and be inspired by the spirit of public interest. Literature is also more important for life than artistic purpose. It is not only the identity of our culture, but also the beat of our life values.)

He writes to connect with the multitude called humanity. The bulk of his readership consists of aspiring youth who are often directionless. I have often heard that many read Chetan Bhagat to improve their English. Similarly I came to know that many readers go to Nishank's work to obtain right directions in life. Nishank has no airs about him and doesn't believe in verbosity and pompousness. His language is the language of the common man and woman, not of the professors teaching in university departments.

> मेरी साहित्य रचना का भी यही परम लक्ष्य और उद्देश्य है। अपनी कहानी में मैं साहित्य के इस धर्म को पूरी संवेदना, स्वच्छंदता और नैसर्गिकता से निभाने की भरसक कोशिश करता रहा हूँ। ताकि हर रचना जनोन्मुखी व जनसरोकारी हो, और पावन गंगा की अविरल जलधारा की तरह लोक-कल्याणकारी भी हो।[9]
>
> (This is the ultimate aim and purpose of my literary pursuits. Through my narratives, I have been trying to fulfil this function of literature with devoted sensitivity, resoluteness and genuineness. I write with passion and my vision is public oriented and welfare for all, and like the continuous flow of the holy Ganges, it is also for the public good.)

Dr. Nishank writes because he feels for the common masses. He recreates them as his characters. The characters speak the language full of empathy for the characters who are people in flesh and blood.

> मेरे भीतर की छटपटाहट ही मेरा साहित्य है। मेरा देखा, महसूस किया और भोगा यथार्थ—संवेदना अनुभूति और अनुभवों से अनुप्राणित। कभी जीवन-मूल्यों की धड़कन बनकर, तो कभी आम आदमी की आवाज बनकर मैं इन्हें सीधे-सरल शब्दों में अपने पाठकों तक पहुँचाने की कोशिश करता रहा हूँ।[10]
>
> (The inner tribulation and turmoil is the foundation of my literature—seen, felt and experienced inspired

by consciousness and enveloped by experiences. I try to present in inornate language of the common men before my readers my experiences as their experiences sometimes as the throbbing life-values and the other time as the grim voice of the oppressed.)

□

3

Dr. Nishank's Literary Value and Appeal

आडंबर तजि कीजिए, गुन संग्रह चितचाय।
छीर रहित गऊ ना बिकै, आनिय घंट बँधाय॥

—वृन्दकवि (1643–1723)

(Abandoning ostentation, accumulate pleasing qualities;
A milkless cow will not be sold by just tying a bell to it.)

The above-mentioned couplet very succinctly and skilfuly underlines the fact that in this consumer-oriented world, nothing can be sold without its value to the buyer. Even literature or a so-called literary work can't be marketed by citing names and showing its ostentation. Long before poet Vrind wrote the above couplet, our Sanskrit poets placed and compiled it in the form of a noble thought for all time to come, as follows:

यदि सन्ति गुणाः पुंसा विकसन्त्येवते स्वयम्।
न हि कस्तूरिकामोदः शपथेन विभाव्यते।।

[If a person has good qualities, they spread by themselves (others get to know about his qualities automatically, he does not have to advertise them). As the fragrance of musk does not need an oath (it proves by itself); it's the fragrance that attracts and not the bulk or pile of something. Similarly, Dr. Nishank's work will speak (बात बोलेगी, हम नहीं—Shamsher Bahadur Singh) for itself.] It will stand the test of time. It will survive or not, is another question altogether.

Of late, I got interested and started reading Nishank's body of work. I wanted to find out the hidden truth of his work. When I was in Libya, I used to give the university students a course in 'Literary Criticism and Theory', but the students always called it 'literary'. For them the word 'literary' was of literary value. In fact, I wanted to see for myself the truth in the statements which were based on anonymous Hindi literature-teachers that Nishank's work is high on patriotism and less on literary value. For me, it was an occasion to discuss the issue of literary value also. It was also an occasion to revisit the very idea of *literary value* and *value* of *literature.*

Let me first discuss the concept of literature and literary value; secondly, we will explore and underline the literariness in Nishank's work. Just as Ben Jonson defines Shakespeare as 'not of an age but for all time', can we define Nishank as 'an author of his time'? The question of literary value, literary survival and literary worth are based on certain judgements. The bases on which our judgements about literary value are made are not very easy to define. T.S. Eliot has used a word repeatedly in his essay *What is a Classic?* (1945) and that word is *maturity*. Do we find that kind of maturity in Nishank's text which Eliot indicates? William Shakespeare, at the end of *King Lear*, uses another word and it is 'ripeness'. Both are similar. I can easily see if a mango is ripe by squeezing it hard but I am unable to do so with a book. The notion of literary value as a sacred spirit will fall to bits and pieces in the twenty-first century if I squeeze it even a little bit. Our discussion about it is only to underline the fact that literary value of a work or an author is based on the readers and their literary sensibilities of a particular time.

Theories of literary value in the West fall into three categories: mimetic, expressive and formalistic. Samuel

Johnson in his *Preface to Shakespeare* (1765) writes, "Nothing can please many, and please long, but just representations of general nature." Coleridge announces an expressive theory of value when he claims that descriptions of the natural world become proof of genius only as far as they are modified by a predominant passion. Russian 'formalism' has defined literary value in terms of the formal linguistic properties of the text. Shklovskii said that the literariness or artfulness of a work of literature, that which makes it an aesthetic object, resides entirely in its devices, which should also form the sole object of literary studies. Literature is a kind of writing which, in the words of the Russian critic, Roman Jacobson, represents an 'organised violence committed on ordinary speech'. Literature transforms and intensifies ordinary language, deviating systematically from everyday speech.

If you aren't unfamiliar with academic literary criticism, you will recollect that during the early 1940s (still going on), literary theorists thought a text could stand on its own. It began with Wimsatt and Beardsley's *The Intentional Fallacy* which argued that the intention of the author (authorial intent) shouldn't matter when interpreting a text. The text will itself make you think something. Later Roland Barthes' seminal essay *Death of the Author* and several other works grouped together was called 'New Criticism'. In schools and colleges and in research, we come across a mode of thinking perpetuated by scholars. In Hindi, the school of Acharya Ramchandra Shukla is still going on. If a student wants to get an 'A', she should apply what 'they' said. The views of others are termed as wrong answers. Can there be only one single professorial way of seeing or interpreting a work?

E.D. Hirsch gives us a way out of this bind with his validity in interpretation. Hirsch makes a point in *Validity in Interpretation'* by making a few observations. The meaning of a text changes even to the author after the work is accomplished. The original intention of the author becomes irrelevant. It doesn't matter what the author means; only what the text says, matters. We can never truly know what the author meant because we are not the author. The author often doesn't even know what his readers may mean of his work or text. Hirsch emphasises that criticism is important because it shows us why a work has value. The reading of a text will also indicate its value, at least its value for the particular reader.

There is an interesting critical distinction that is worth considering here that E.D. Hirsch makes in *Validity in Interpretation.* He distinguishes between *meanings*—what the writer intends the work to mean—and *significance*—what a text signifies or means to you, personally. The first is objective; the second, is subjective. You can make a similar distinction on value. When a critic calls something an 'instant classic' or the like, he is proclaiming and attaching value-to-him, not objective value, which can only come over time and with gradual recognition.

A new generation of critics that came to prominence in the sixties and seventies and are still considered prominent (Jacques Derrida, Roland Barthes, Michel Foucault and Julia Kristeva) have different views about literary value. Frank Kermode, in his book *The Classic* (1975) says that a book or text that speaks to all generations can be called 'timeless' and 'a literary classic'. The earlier critics, such as F.R. Leavis and I.A. Richards, assigned to the arts and literature a moral purpose but the new brand of theorists condemned it and termed it as 'orthodox'. As we move into 'post-theory' era, a new generation of young readers emerges and it dismissing the very idea of 'literary value'. There is a need to defend literary value for the sake of longevity of literature.

Literature, as the Welsh poet Dylan Thomas once said, is a 'sullen art'. Bound between the covers of a book, the writer's craft is made up of black marks that lie silent on the page. Yet, literature can also empower us to 'live deep and suck the marrow out of life' says Henry David Thoreau. Let me add here an interesting dialogue from a very famous English film. The film *Dead Poets Society* (1989) is one of the most enduring and loved pictures ever made about teaching the humanities. In the film, actor Robin Williams, in the guise of an English teacher, John Keating, says that he reads literature because he is a member of the human race and the human race is filled with passion! Medicine, law, banking are necessary to sustain life; but poetry, romance, love, beauty—these are what we stay alive for. The actor repeating the dialogues given to him was praised by everyone; but the fact is that he didn't say anything new and amazing.

Great literature, according to German poet Ranier Maria Rilke, makes us aware that 'we must change our life.' W.B. Yeats said, 'Man lives and dies between two eternities, that of race and of soul'. Likewise literature too lives and dies between two eternities—the infinitude of the individual work of literature—be it a poem, short story or novel—and the infinitude of world literature which, like an underground river or the underground waters that are an invisible envelope in a living whole. 'A glass of water to drink or a plunge into a river in spate!' said K.R. Shrinivasa Iyengar while delivering the key-note address in a conference at Guntur in 1974. We believe that a man taking a dip in a river can't take the dip in the same water twice. Kabir indicates that language flows like water and what is literature but language made to order (tailor-made) by the author. It is amazing but true that the word 'text' has been taken from Latin root 'textum'. It was basically used for fabric. The word *text* has its origins in Quintilian's book on speeches with the statement that 'after you have chosen your words, they must be weaved together into a fine and delicate fabric.' It is more than a coincidence that Kabir has been a weaver by profession and weaver of texts without any pretext of pedantry (मसि कागद छूओ नहीं कलम गहि नहीं हाथ). Kabir is a great poet and his literary value far exceeds the vagaries of time.

What we call 'literary' or 'literature' depends on various factors. Indian *Theory of Literature* has its own tradition and thinking about literary value. The Western criticism and theory is slightly different. However, the impact of Western

(English) education for long has influenced Hindi intellectuals also to reformulate their views about literature and a selective exchange with Western criticism along with a selective view of Indian literary criticism has not been an unfamiliar territory for us. Andrew Bennett and Nicholas Royle's lively, original and highly readable book, *An Introduction to Literature Criticism and Theory* present the Western point of view as follows:

> *"Literature in a sense does not exist. It has no essence. It is not a case of X being a literary text, and Y being non-literary. Literariness is more spectral and elusive. Any text conventionally considered as literary (Geoffrey Chaucer's The Wife of Bath's Prologue and Tale, say) can be read as non-literary (for example, as an account of female sexuality in the Middle Ages); and conversely, any text conventionally considered as non-literary (a political speech, say) can be read as literary [(for example, in terms of an enactment of the strange ways of language, the workings of metaphor and other rhetorical figures]."*[1]

Prof. Krishna Rayan, perhaps the only contemporary Indian critic to develop a theory of Indian literature by putting to use ancient Sanskrit Poetics, in an essay published in an edited volume, *Indian Literary Tradition*, says that literature is distinguished from other forms of linguistic discourse by virtue of the complexity of literary language and that complexity arises from the ability of literature to be 'suggestive'. Indian literary tradition considers that literariness can be found in the text when the dominance of unstated implied meaning is found. In the opening verse of the *Dhvanyalok*, the 9th-century Sanskrit classic of literary theory, *kavyastma dhavanih* (*dhvani*, i.e. suggested meaning: suggestion is the essence of poetry or more widely of literature). In other words, if anyone writes with a view to suggesting something beyond words, his work is worthwhile and can be called 'literary'. Language loaded with suggestive meaning is literature.

Though discussed thoroughly around the world, the truth is that amidst literary circles, it is still not clear what it is. The reader and the critic, both look at a work for different reasons. It is the critic who tries hard to decide and place a work in proper perspective. It will be worthwhile to look at these different but important perspectives before relying on the act of reading by an average reader.

Paratext

When a book is written and handed over to the publisher and the set of editors etc. gives the green signal and it is published, the reader and others, each receive a copy of it. The former generally buys it and the latter ordinarily gets a complimentary copy, free of cost. The value of books is constructed through *paratext* by the printer as directed by the publisher and his team. Paratext, in other words, is the look of the book. Through a close reading of its paratext, one can easily understand how a sense of literary value is produced. Paratext is all of the information that surrounds a story and that creates expectations about the story. Thus, it is involved in the continuous process of creating literary value. But none of these markers are truly the indicators of the literary value of the book, though in the present-day scenario, literary value is created and marketed. When a book is published by a so-called reputed publisher or a body of government agency (Sahitya Akademi, Bharatiya Jnanpith and National Book Trust, etc.) it gets some kind of value. This value has nothing to do with the book's real worth and its lasting literary value. A very recent example of how publishers create value and market the book can be gauged by the activities of *Hind Yugm* and its publisher, who created a slogan 'नईवाली हिंदी' (It is similar to those days when *khadi boli* was being marketed by saying, 'हिंदी नई चाल में ढली।') An aura is created around a book and its author and if the book has some worth too, it will have value also.

Let me give an example from a text by Dr. Nishank. I have a novel written by him in my hand. The novel is titled *Nishant*. It was published in 2008. The title of the book rhymes with the novelist's name. I look at the blurb for paratext to know more about the novel. I have heard this name before in connection with a 1975 film, directed by Shyam Benegal. This film focuses on the power of the rural elite and the sexual exploitation of women during the time of feudalism in India. At the back cover of the novel, there is detailed introduction of the author and the name of the publisher. I look for some information about the novel but on the blurb I get the appreciative recommendations about the author as follows:

> निशांत
>
> हिंदी साहित्यकारों में डॉ. रमेश पोखरियाल 'निशंक' ने देदीप्यमान नक्षत्र की तरह अपनी उपस्थिति दर्ज की है। 'निशंक' की निरंतर अबाधगति से चली आ रही साहित्य-यात्रा हिंदी की समृद्धि और श्रीवृद्धि कर एक नया आयाम स्थापित करेगी। ऐसी रचनाएँ लोगों में देशभक्ति का जज्बा पैदा करती हैं। सामाजिक क्षेत्र में सक्रिय रहने वाले डॉ. निशंक ने अब तक डेढ़ दर्जन से भी अधिक पुस्तकों का प्रकाशन उनकी प्रखरता, संकल्पशीलता, रचनाधर्मिता तथा संवेदनशीलता का प्रमाण देती है। निश्चित ही 'निशंक' ने ऐसी कृतियों की रचना कर राष्ट्र का गौरव बढ़ाया है।
>
> —डॉ. ए.पी.जे. अब्दुल कलाम, पूर्वराष्ट्रपति, भारत[2]

This is strange on the part of the publisher that the blurb indicates to its readers the novel *Nishant,* but tells about the novelist 'Nishank'.

> (Among Hindi litterateurs, Dr. Ramesh Pokhriyal 'Nishank' has made his presence known as a grand constellation. The literary journey of Nishank at the uninterrupted pace will establish a new dimension by enrichment and growth of Hindi. Such creations instil patriotism in the people. Dr. Nishank, who has been active in the field, has published more than one and a half dozen books so far, giving proof of his sharpness, determination, creativity and sensitivity. Certainly 'Nishank' has made the nation proud by creating such works.)

Similarly, the blurb cites one of the well-known poet-politicians and tells us about the novelist, but the reader gets no information about the contents of the novel.

> सक्रिय राजनीति में रहते हुए भी जिस प्रखरता से डॉ. निशंक साहित्य के क्षेत्र में लगातार संघर्षरत हैं, यह आम आदमी के बस की बात नहीं है। मुझे डॉ. निशंक की संघर्षशीलता और दृढ़ इच्छाशक्ति पर पूर्ण विश्वास है कि वे अपने राजनैतिक जीवन की व्यस्तताओं के उपरांत भी अपनी लेखनी के माध्यम से आम जनमानस की भावनाओं को उभारकर समाज और देश के सामने ऐसे प्रश्न खड़े करते रहेंगे, जिनके उत्तर के लिए कभी-न-कभी जिम्मेदार व्यक्तियों को अपने कर्तव्यों का एहसास जरूर हो जाएगा।
>
> —श्री अटल बिहारी वाजपेयी, पूर्व प्रधानमंत्री[3]

> (Despite being in the active politics, the vigour with which Dr. Nishank is constantly struggling and creating new space for himself in the realm of literature can't be attained by an ordinary man. I have full faith in the struggle and strong will-power of Dr. Nishank that he will continue to raise such questions and issues before our society and country through his writings so that the reactions and sentiments of the masses are made known to the people who are responsible to mitigate their woes also realise their duties towards them.)
>
> —Atal Bihari Vajpayee, late Prime Minister of India

The novel '*Nishank*' has no foreword or preface and the reader has to go straight to the novel. The publisher seems to suggest that the reader is going to read 'Nishank' and not the novel *Nishant*. This act of negligence is not new in the realm of literary presentations as the creator is considered more important than the creation. This is also reflected in the literary criticism and review-articles as the critics tend to eulogise the authors and not their literary output. For instance, Dr. Ravi Kumar Gond has written a critical piece on the novel which starts with these words:

> सन् 15 अगस्त, 1959 को गाँव पिनानी (पौढ़ी गढ़वाल), उत्तराखंड प्रदेश में जन्म लेने वाले डॉ. रमेश पोखरियाल 'निशंक' न केवल एक बेहतरीन कवि हैं, बल्कि एक कुशल कथाकार भी हैं। उनके द्वारा लिखित उपन्यास 'निशांत' स्त्री-संघर्ष का दस्तावेज है।[4]
>
> (Born on 15 August, 1959 in village Pinani (Pauri Garhwal), Uttarakhand, Dr. Ramesh Pokhriyal 'Nishank' is not only a great poet, but also a skilled narrator. The novel *Nishant* written by him is a document of women-struggle.)

This is the standard procedure in literary criticism in Hindi and is largely inspired by the conventional-mode propagated by Acharya Ram Chandra Shukla and his ilk. In the Western world, theorists, such as Gayatri Chakravorty Spivak, Henry Louis Gates Jr. and Edward Said, for example, have transformed the nature of contemporary literary studies and criticism. Edward Said argues for 'contrapuntal reading' whereby, in reading a text, one 'open[s] it out both to what went into it and to what its author excluded.'[5] Such readings are based upon the premise that any literary fiction refers to or depicts a theme that has been taken from the actual world. When Nishank writes a novel or a short story, he draws his characters and incidents from actual people, places and institutions, religious and social practices and so on. He puts them in his use according to his 'structure of reference and attitude'. The reader should keep in mind that this structure should be his base also from which a contrapuntal reading will proceed smoothly. No one can and should read him without this stance. For instance, the novel is said to be the depiction of the struggle of Mitali, but it is titled as *Nishant*. We find that the female lead of the novel named Mitali is ever grateful to the male protagonist, Nishant.

> इस चिड़िया को तो तुमने ही एहसास कराया कि इसके पंख हैं, वरना वह तो उड़ना ही भूल गई थी। इसकी उड़ान की दिशा एवं पंखों को ताकत तो तुमने ही दी है।[6]

> (You made this bird realise that it has wings; otherwise she had forgotten to fly. You only have given strength to my flight its direction and wings.)

Such a study limits the over-all perspective of the novel. Once you read this novel with the changed title, its force immediately alters. It is no longer a novel of 'a man helping his better-half'. The novel's engagement with her relatives and their response with social and political ramifications will enhance its literary value. We all know that a woman reading a novel is different from a man reading the same novel. I have no proof but my gut feeling is that a large number of Dr. Nishank's readers are women.

Who Decides Literary Value of a Work?

There are writers and writers on one side and readers and critics, on the other. Once a book is published and a large body of readers from far and wide read and appreciate it, the critics start saying favourable things; it is possible that the book gets its rightful place. The key element here is time. Of course, there have been instant classics and every day we hear publishers claim a book as a 'best-seller'. As I see it, it takes time to determine if a given work will last and underscore its literary value. Like fashions and films, writers also have a shelf-life. Yes, some critics make and mar the book and its author. In English, it was Harold Bloom and in Hindi, Namvar Singh, who used to play this game effortlessly. Invariably, it is the critics' subjective taste and that taste is not infallible.

I have always been an avid reader of Hindi and English literature. My idea of literature and literary value has been formed and framed by my study and personal experience in the field. An anecdote is often heard in literary circles and usually scoffed at. Once during an interview for the post of a professor, one of the interviewers dismissed a book written by a candidate thus, "I haven't come across this book before." The candidate very curtly replied, "I didn't send any free copy to anyone." If I write the names of these two Hindi stalwarts, they will get offended, but it is true. The literary merit of a book is decided by a few selected ones associated with certain academies, universities and isms.

Martin Heidegger once said, "Even mere ism is a misunderstanding and the death of history." Acharya Ramchandra Shukla wrote *History of Hindi Literature* (1929), which to this day remains the best book in Hindi for its kind and a model for others to follow. Acharya Shukla also remarked when he sensed that leaning towards an 'ism' like 'Marxism' is distorting the very liberty taken by poets is being unconsciously curtailed.

> कुछ दिनों में लोग कविता न लिखकर, 'वाद' लिखने लगते हैं।
>
> (Poets start writing '*ism*' and not the poems after a while.)

For so many years, the JNU brigade decided many things. There are self-styled professors and *acharyas* who try to dominate by labelling works according to their personal whims and fancies and dogged ideals. The fight was seldom between the Left and the Right, but between different shades of red. "The people from the literati and upper classes from Andhra Pradesh, Maharashtra, West Bengal, Tamil Nadu, etc., who came to the university both as faculty as well as students, gave the university a profile quite different from that of any other university in modern India."[7] This kind of profile and leaning changed the Indian academicians. Red became the colour and saffron was highly detested. Some of the Hindi scholars of such institutions changed the very course of Hindi criticism in India. One fine morning, a great critic takes up a novel and declares to the TV viewers:

> मुझे इस उपन्यास के शिल्प ने मुख्य रूप से आकर्षित किया, जिस तरह कथानक का कलात्मक ढाँचा बनता है, वह कथा-साहित्य में नया प्रयोग करने की कोशिश है, वरना आदि, मध्य और अंत के रूप में कथा कहने वाले उपन्यास भरे पड़े हैं।[8]

(I have been greatly attracted by this novel's texture. The way the artful structure of the narrative formed is an attempt to experiment in a fresh way; otherwise, there are novels in abundance where the story is told with a beginning, middle and an end.)

Once an author gets such a critical review from a person of eminence, the literary value of the work soars in the sky. The beauty of the sentence quoted above is that it can be applied to any novel.

This is in relation to these so-called academicians. You would appreciate if I cite Dr. Nishank's reply to reporters in Haldwani about protests against amended Citizenship Act across university campuses, "Universities are centres of learning where the country's future is in the making. We cannot let them become *addas* of politics."[9] Badri Narayan, professor and director of G.B. Pant Social Science Institute, Prayagraj comments that Nishank is struggling not only to transform the nature of our education system but also its perspectives and philosophy. He is also trying to resolve language and identity issues and bureaucratic challenges. The balancing and harmonising of two jobs and vocations is a feat Dr. Nishank has been performing with dexterity and élan and can be better viewed by more than one million followers of his Facebook profile. Dr. Nishank is a minister who spares some time to write something literary also. He religiously posts one of his poems for readers to read and get inspired.

To put it differently, it is a fact universally admitted that literary value does not include the values expressed or implied in a text but refers specifically to how one can attribute value to a text in terms of its value to 'civilisation', a culture, a society, or a particular group of people. This particular group of people sometimes plays a partisan game or has a vision coloured by so many factors. The English critic, Cyril Connolly, seems to substantiate this idea when he writes that the function of the critic is to stand at the gates of Parnassus where men of letters line up for admission to immortality and as each one steps forward to bash him over the head with a club.

Empathy as Literary Value

Sensibility refers to an acute perception of or responsiveness towards something, such as the emotions of another. It is different from sentimentality and is akin to empathy, which is the capacity to understand or feel what another person is experiencing from within his or her frame of reference, that is, the capacity to place oneself in another's position.

When I started teaching English literature in 1975, literary study was being replaced by ELT and linguistics. I have been witnessing literature's gradual decline since then. Now I usually pray to God that I should leave this earth before its complete extinction. At present, the study of literature is intrinsically valuable as an end in itself only. The market of literature or the value of literature is shrinking. The professors of literature will very soon become endangered species. Prof. Michael Fischer, in a well-meaning paper '*Literature and Empathy*' (2017), says that only the empathy in defence of literature can save us. The new breed of CEOs who want 'empathy' in their resume must get it from literature. When T.S. Eliot called poetry 'a superior amusement', he was indicating its value as empathy. Poets and authors are churning out books in the fond hope of getting readership, but in vain. The writers claim that they have empathy in abundance, and the readers go to them to strengthen their empathetic imagination.

Since the discovery of 'mirror neurons', various disciplines have devoted themselves to empathy, stressing its social relevance. Empathy is inseparable from narrative to understand others' feelings. Reading is claimed to stimulate our emotional intelligence. Recently, some pioneering work in neuroscience has begun to suggest that the power of literature is the power of alterity, creating the possibility of encountering the other in a form not easily recoverable or not easily assailable to the self. Our cognition is shaped not just by what we read, but how we read. Test subject, Matt Langione, a doctoral candidate at Berkeley in the US, leisurely read a novel in the mock scanning room. Researchers found that blood flow in the brain increases during such leisurely reading. But when he read the same novel more closely, the flow of blood was in different areas of the brain. It was found that close reading of a literary text created some distinct vibrations and flow of blood. What the literary theorists called *samvedna* (hypnotic trance) is a cognitive transformation of the reader. If a text is able to do so, it's very much literary.

We know that there are many classics in Hindi. *Aakar granths* (canonical works of everlasting literary value) are a set of texts whose value and readability have borne the test of time. *Ramcharitmanas* is one such book. It is our cherished literature and Tulsidas is the poet par excellence. But there have been hundreds of *Ramayanas* and each one of these books is worth the weight of gold. It is not the subjective literary value but the objective literary value which is the result of a consensus of opinion over time. That is why it is called 'objective'. Can anyone evaluate *Ramcharitmanas* as a poor work on the grounds that it doesn't contribute well to the Dalit discourse of our time? Similarly, can one reject all the other *Ramayanas* written by so many known and unknown poets as inferior or of less literary value as they are not discussed in any history of Hindi literature? They all deserve appreciation and praise. *Pariksha Guru* is a great first novel as Acharya Ramchandra Shukla mentioned it, but *Devrani Jethani ki Kahani* is far greater as it is not an imitation of any '*videshi angrezi dhang*'(foreign English manner). Both are written in a realistic mode for depicting the contemporary social reality; both have literary value as well. *Pariksha Guru* has literary value for Acharya Shukla but the other novel has the same for Prof. Gopal Rai, who unearthed the novel *Devrani Jethani ki Kahani* from oblivion and spoke volumes about it in his *History of Hindi Novels*. As the literary art of memory receives, retains and orders selective works, many remarkable texts might not stand the test of time or might have been overlooked, or unavailable and lost in the haze of antiquity. This selectivity in Hindi literature can be gauged when the critic Ramswarup Chaturvedi concludes and writes the last paragraph of his history of Hindi literature, *Hindi Sahitya aur Samvedna ka Vikas*:

> गृहस्थी और परिवार का जीवन लोक-अग्नि की पहली आँच है, जिससे तप-गलकर श्रद्धा स्वर्ण-प्रतिमा जैसी निखरती है। तब यह अचरज नहीं कि हिंदी के तीन बड़े रचनाकार तुलसीदास, मैथिलीशरण गुप्त, प्रेमचंद परिवार की मर्यादा/मरजाद का चित्रण करके ही जन-प्रिय हुए हैं। हमारी भाषा और संस्कृति ने जीवन के एक-एक संबंध को अलग-अलग सँजोकर रखा है, और यहीं से हमने विरुद्धों के सामंजस्य की सीख ली है।[10]
> (Domesticity and family life is the initial flame of community-fire in which *shraddha* (*Shraddha* is one of the prominent characters in the epic poem *Kamayani*, composed by Jai Shankar Prasad.) shines like a golden statue. Then it is not surprising that three great Hindi writers—Tulsidas, Maithilisharan Gupt and Premchand—have got popularity only by depicting the dignity/*marjad* of a family ... Our language and culture have beautifully maintained each and every relation of life differently, and only for there we have learnt the lesson of juxtaposition of the opposites.)

These lines can provide us a clear indication of *literariness* and *literature* and also of *literary value*. The two bright stars of Hindi literary firmament—Acharya Ramchandra Shukla and Acharya Ramswarup Chaturvedi firmly suggest that the literary value of a work lies in its *samvedna*. Let me give you these thoughts using the usual system of enumeration.

(a) The text should adhere to the tenets of our tradition.
(b) There should be confluence of thought (*samanvya sadhna*) and juxtaposition of opposites.

(c) Family and the values enshrined in it should be followed.

(d) The language used should also show the blend of all the languages included in the Hindi family.

Dr. Nishank is not only aware of the value of *samvedna* as the foundation of literary creation, but also realises that the written word gets its life through it.

> संवेदना साहित्य का 'मूल आधार' ही नहीं, 'आत्मा' भी है। जैसे उर्वरता बिना धरती 'बाँझ' है, वैसे ही संवेदना बगैर साहित्य निष्प्राण होता है। यही संवेदनशीलता हमें मानवीय मूल्यों एवं मानवीय रिश्तों से जोड़ती है और जीवन को उसकी समग्रता में अनुभव कराती है। साहित्य इसी वेदना, संवेदना, अनुभूति, और अनुभवों से अनुप्राणित होता आया है। यही संवेदना साहित्य को सजग एवं सार्थक बनाती है। जीवन-मूल्यों के लिए मेरे अंदर की छटपटाहट इसी संवेदना की देन है। यही संवेदना मुझे जन-जन से जोड़ती आई है, उनका सहयोगी और सहभागी बनाती आई है। मेरी रचनाओं का संबल और शक्ति यही जन-चेतना रही है। मुझे जनोन्मुखी एवं जनसरोकारी रचनाओं के लिए यही संवेदना प्रेरित करती रही है। इसे ही मैं सच्चे साहित्य की सार्थकता मानता हूँ और इसी को समर्पित हूँ।[11]
>
> (Sensitivity is not only the 'basic foundation' of literature but also its 'soul'. Just as the earth is 'infertile' without its 'fertility', literature is soulless without any sensitivity. This sensitivity connects us to human values and human relationships and makes life worth living in its totality. Literature has been greatly enthused by this pain, sensation, feeling, and experiences. Both sensitivity and sentimentality makes literature watchful and meaningful. The understanding in me for life values is the result of this innate feeling. This has also connected me with people by making them as my partners in the voyage of discovery. I have always been inspired by these sentiments for the welfare of the people and public-oriented works. I consider this to be the true meaning of literature and I am dedicated to it.)

I would like to point out here that Dr. Nishank is an author and politician, both. As a politician, he must be a reader of his work to get *samvedna* (empathy) for the masses. He meets ordinary and extra-ordinary people around him and then imaginatively enters their lives to write about them with empathy and concern. Therefore, when he writes or is in his act of writing, he realises their human rights and concerns. In this way, as a democratic leader, Dr. Nishank becomes his own instructor. He becomes more humane than before as he is capable of listening to others' points of view. This impact of the common men on him is not restricted to his literary output, but also to his humanitarian services and political acumen.

We need the inspiring and motivational words of others to wake us up. Even Hanuman, the very epitome of wisdom, wanted a Jambvant. Dr. Nishank's *samvedna* for others, which is reflected in his works, becomes a soothing balm for persons in pain and distress. His work has a humanising effect. Once we, as readers of Dr. Nishank's work, get that feeling of empathy or *samvedna* and start inhabiting others' points of view, we can also be instrumental in making the society a just one to live.

Dr. Nishank's Literary Value

Now let us turn to Dr. Nishank and his work. What is its literary value? One Kritika Sharma quotes an anonymous former President of the *Sahitya Kala Akademi*: "I have been a part of a literary body, but I have never come across any work by Ramesh Pokhriyal. Maybe it doesn't have any literary value." This is no answer. One who has been a part of literary body is expected to be well-read and well-informed. The former President should have asked a former member about his work before pronouncing such rash judgement. I know that a former member of Sahitya Akademi has not only read Nishank well but also written a well-researched book, *Kathakar Nishank ke Upanyaso me Jeevan Mulya* on him. I have no hesitation to reveal his name. He is Dr. Yogendra Nath Sharma 'Arun' and his name needs no introduction in India.

As discussed before, Dr. Yogendra Nath Sharma 'Arun' is one of the finest teachers of Hindi literature, poet and writer and critic of sharp sensibilities. In his distinguished career, he had nurtured and nourished many students into researchers. He has been still very active in the field. Dr. Ramesh Pokhriyal 'Nishank' can claim that he has been lucky to receive critical appreciation from him. This appreciation is not based on anything but on his more than 10 novels which were thoroughly read, discussed and placed in the right perspective. He recognised Dr. Nishank's literary value and in a way, he has been instrumental in letting the world know about him. What was Ram Vilas Sharma for Nirala, Yogendra Nath Sharma 'Arun' is for Dr. Nishank. Dr. Arun has the following words to comment on his literary value:

> अत्यंत सुखद संयोग यह है कि डॉ. 'निशंक' राजनीति के साथ-साथ साहित्य के क्षेत्र में भी अत्यंत सफल और लोकप्रिय हुए हैं। ईश्वर ने डॉ. निशंक को बहुआयामी रचना-प्रतिभा प्रदान की है। जहाँ वे कवि के रूप में 'राष्ट्रवादी चिंतन' को सशक्त अभिव्यक्ति देते हैं, वहीं उनके उपन्यासों में पर्वतीय जीवन की इंद्रधनुषी झाँकियाँ देखकर पाठक का मन आल्हाद से भर उठता है। कहानीकार के रूप में डॉ. 'निशंक' अपने आसपास बिखरे अनुभवों को शब्दों में गूँथ-गूँथकर मनोहारी अभिव्यक्ति देकर पाठक का मन मोह लेते हैं।[12]
>
> (It is a very joyful coincidence that Dr. Nishank has become very successful and popular in the field of politics as well as literature. Almighty God has given Dr. 'Nishank' a multi-faceted talent. While he provides strong expression to 'nationalist thought' as a poet, the reader's mind is filled with joy after observing the lofty peaks of the Himalayas and mountain life in his novels. As a story-teller, Dr. Nishank captivates the reader by his expressive depiction through word-pictures of the myriad expressions scattered around him.)

You shouldn't find any contradiction in my statement when I say that a certain critic labels a book as *literary or* otherwise just for its sake, without going deep into it, and another one finds in Nishank's work literariness after going through his books as a reader-critic. Critical response is always welcome but it is the reader-response that is worthy of praise and admiration.

Reader Response as Literary Value

A piece of literature appeals to us only when it calls into activity the same powers of sympathy and imagination in us as that went into writing it creatively. Reading is one of the few distinctively human activities that set us apart from the rest of the animal kingdom. But there is no solid reason to read a literary text. It serves no purpose; has no function. When I read a fictional narrative or wish to read a novel or short story by Dr. Nishank, I read it for my own pleasure. This pleasure I get because I am able to identify with a character, narrator, author or situation. If it is not possible, I may abandon it. I may not read it any further. Reading is a way in which I come to know myself. I think even the author will be able to write a novel or a short story only when he/she identifies with it, in one way or the other. The empathetic function in fiction is accomplished via the writer's relation to his characters. It's also accomplished via the writer's relation to his readers. The relationship between the reader and the writer creates a bond that is a marker of literary value of the text. The mark of a good reader is the ability to read a text and recognise that it is very good or great, while at the same time saying that it doesn't interest him or her in the slightest. It's an exercise in objectivity that is worth pursuing.

Ronald Barthes in his book *The Pleasure of the Text* (1970) calls it 'disavowal'. It means that the reader keeps thinking, 'I know these are only words, but all the same...' This is similar to Coleridge's idea of 'willing suspension of disbelief'. 'Reading is the sole means, by which we slip, involuntarily, often helplessly, into another's skin, another's voice, another's soul.' Joyce Carol Oates is not off the mark when she says this to underline the value of a reader's response. Similarly when the Nobel Prize-winner Italian poet and novelist Salvador Kwasimodo (1901-1968) says in an interview given to *The New York Times* (14 May, 1960), he underlines the value and worth of the reader and in a way puts both the poet and the reader, ont the same pedestal. Poetry is the revelation of a feeling that the poet believes to be interior and personal (but) which the reader recognises as his own.

So much scholarly work about literature has little to do with human impulses that are the primary reasons that people read literature and poetry. A story, a novel, or a poem should be personally meaningful to the reader. The traditional purpose of literature has been just 'to delight and instruct'. If these two purposes are met by Dr. Nishank's work, it has not only literary value but also literary merit. Dr. Harivansh Rai Bachchan writes:

> कविता की प्रजा दो प्रकार की होती है—एक वह, जो कविता को बौद्धिक संवेदन देती है, जो उससे तटस्थ रहती है, उसे कौतूहल की दृष्टि से देखती है और दूसरी वह, जो उसे हार्दिक सहानुभूति देती है, उसकी भावधारा में बहती है, उसे अपने प्राणों में रचा-बसा लेती है। आपको अपनी अभिव्यक्ति का अंग बनाकर मैं केवल अपनी रुचि बतलाना चाहता हूँ कि मुझे कविता की किस प्रकार की प्रजा पसंद है।[13]
>
> (There are two types of subjects of poetry. One, who gives an intellectual sensation to the poem, which is neutral, looks at with curiosity, and the other who gives her heartfelt sympathy flows into her sentiment. Makes him live in his life. By making you a part of my expression, I just want to show my inclination in what kind of subjects I like in poetry.)

Reader-response theory is based on the assumption that a literary work takes place in the mutual relationship between the reader and the text. According to this theory, the meaning is constructed through a transaction between the reader and the text within a particular context. Norman Holland argues that 'interpretation is a function of identity' and that 'all of us, as we read, use the literary work to symbolise and finally to replicate ourselves.'[14] Therefore, when a reader reads Nishank's books, he/she finds it attractive and valuable on the basis of his reading and understanding. This is also to be noted that the community of readers who have read Nishank's novels, short stories and selections of poetry and later wrote their interpretative texts with a view to underlining his literary value have this to say:

> प्रमुख पाश्चात्य काव्यशास्त्री लोंजाइनस की मान्यता है कि किसी साहित्यिक कृति में उदात्त तत्त्व का अवतरण तभी संभव है, जब कि उसके रचनाकार के अपने जीवन और व्यक्तित्व में औदात्य विद्यमान हो। यह उक्ति डॉ. निशंक के व्यक्तित्व और कृतित्व पर पूरी तरह लागू होती है। अर्थात् उनके व्यक्तित्व में विद्यमान औदार्य और औदात्य ही उनके कृतित्व में उदात्त तत्त्व के रूप में प्रतिबिंबित होता है।[15]
>
> (A leading Western literary critic Longinus holds the view that the creation of the sublime element in a literary work is possible only if its creator has greatness and enormity in his life and personality. This quote is fully applicable to Dr. Nishank's personality and work. That is, the sublime character of his personality is reflected as a sublime element in his work also.)

Dr. Rishabha Deo Sharma, a doyen of Sanskrit Poetics, here uses the Western concept of the sublime and is almost accurate in his realisation. K.R. Srinivasa Iyengar also once said that there appears to be no parallel to the Western concept of the sublime but 'an exhilaration and enjoyment that is more like spiritual realisation' is very much present in Indian literature. Only after I read with great interest the theorisation of the sublime from Longinus to Kant again, I was able to understand the wisdom with which Dr. Rishabha Deo Sharma applied it to Dr. Nishank's work.

Dr. Nishank wants to make everyone culturally enlightened, while he emphasises on the person to be endowed with qualities like objectivity, service and love. Sublimity is the best quality of human heart that transforms manhood into Godhead. Love and humane outlook constitute the cornerstone of noble hearts that transform a sense of righteousness in the heart. It is evident that the combined feeling of love and service to mankind is very important for Dr. Nishank as an author. It is also interesting to note that the influence of Swami Vivekananda and his magnanimity on Dr. Nishank is great. He has written a few books on him.

Let me cite the opinion of Prof. Harishankar Mishr of Lucknow University to substantiate my views in this regard. He says that according to poetess Mahadevi Verma, the writer and his writing are not poles apart. If you weigh the one, the other is evaluated itself. Dr. Mishr evaluates Dr. Nishank's persona with his work and finds that he is an author of immense sensibilities.

> 'निशंक' जी के व्यक्तित्व और कृतित्व के युगपत विश्लेषण से मुझे यह स्पष्ट हुआ कि वे व्युत्पन्न और संवेदना-संपन्न साहित्यकार हैं। उन्हें लोक और शास्त्र की पक्की परख और गहरी अनुभूति है।[16]

—वदनं प्रसाद सदनंसदयं हृदयं सुधामुचोवाचः।
करणं परोपकरणं येषाम, केषामनतेवन्द्यः॥ — *भर्तृहरि*

The above *shloka* is cited by the learned professor to underline the quality of Dr. Nishank and his work and according to him, Dr. Nishank's erudite wisdom is beyond doubt. Only when I devoted an entire year and more in solitary confinement due to the outbreak of Corona virus and read Dr. Nishank's texts I could find some justification in saying to myself:

> *"For Dr. Nishank, writing is sadhna. It is not a profession but a vocation. That is why he has been writing for a long time. For him, writing is a spiritual experience. It is not an intellectual adventure and escape from reality. It is the fruit of sadhna for sadbhavna for the masses."*

Don't you think that a man with a lofty character, who writes with *sadhna* and *sadbhavna*, must have great literary value?

There are some readers who read him or are tempted to read him in terms of power relations. It is a fact that Dr. Nishank is presently a central minister and politician. He is associated with a powerful political party. There are many readers who may go to his text to read the inherent meaning of his text with a view to underlining the message of his party and politics. It is not strange as literary texts have very often used and read in terms of power relations in accordance with Michel Foucault's suggestion that 'power is everywhere', even in reading a text. Nishank's reading demands not only a 'faithful' reading; it also demands an individual response.

To put it differently, reading is at once singular and general. Nishank's literary value can both be determined by those singular readers who together make a community of readers. Those who wish to read him, to find out traces of his party line just to indicate others that Dr. Nishank's writing is biased, will be able to find something according to their tastes and liking. The others will find that his politics is the politics of brotherhood that encompasses the entire length and breadth of this world. His poetry is not only for delight but also for education. He has a mission to educate the youth to let their boundless energy channelised for the welfare and development of the country. Nishank writes:

> मातृभूमि, देशभक्ति की उदात्त भावना से ही 'विश्वबंधुत्व' की भावना साकार हो सकती है तथा श्रेष्ठ नैतिक मूल्यों की स्थापना भी हो सकती है, यहीं इन कविताओं और गीतों का आधार है और सदैव रहा है।[17]
>
> (Only through the sublime patriotic sensibility for the motherland, the feeling of international brotherhood can materialise and this is the foundation of these songs and poems as ever.)

This book is the product of my reading of Dr. Nishank and as a reader I have tried to draw as much as I could. One of the veiled aims of this book, as you can understand, is to inspire you to read him through and through or as you deem appropriate. That is why your reading is going to be a programmed response, conditioned by my reading. To put it differently, all of us are interrelated and interconnected as readers helping and influencing each other.

From Literary Value to Values in Literature

Man is a value-seeking, value-fulfilling, concept-forming animal. The meaning and values of civilisation are not easy to define. There are values: disvalues, un-values or counter values also. Radhakamal Mukerjee (different from Radhakumud Mukherjee), in his seminal work, *The Social Structure of Values* (1950), looks at values in two forms: the philosophical one and the social one. He believes that social science has an obligation to fix the good and determine the values of the society. He seeks to set up a trans-social, religious system of ideal values as the solution for our 'disturbed ways'. Mukherjee identifies moral power with social intelligence. For him, it is the means of achieving an equitable status arrangement in our society. It is "the only hope of the weak against the all-powerful, the solace of the vanquished against the victors, the pride of the outcasts against the elite."[18] According to him, values are derived from life, from environment, from self, society and culture, and beyond all, from the ideal, transcendent dimension of human existence and experience.

When we look at 'value' in another form—the literary value, we associate it with culture and place it with the cultural norms of our social life. Samuel Johnson said in his *Preface to Shakespeare* that "the only test of literary greatness is length of duration and continuance of esteem." Moreover, a book may be considered great if it meets three criteria. The first is universality. A great book speaks to people across many ages—affecting, inspiring and changing readers far removed from the time and place in which it was written. Second, it has a Central One Idea (COI) and themes that address matters of enduring importance. And third, it features noble language. A great book is written in beautiful language that enriches the mind and elevates the soul. We find that the bulk of Dr. Nishank's literary output is valuable as a contribution to our literary wealth. There is little doubt that his literary value will stand the test of time too. Secondly, some of the age-old literary values may have become defunct because at this age we are witnessing 'the death of the so-called literary world'. In the changing world, values are not a fixed set of criteria and the digital age is changing our set of values too. Nishank's work will also be valued and read for the contemporary values it tries to impart. Therefore, it can be said that the value—literary value—of Dr. Nishank's work will be judged and measured from time to time by the readers reading him according to their orientation and cognitive beliefs.

We have been saying for a long time that the readers of literary texts directly or indirectly pick up some universal values and educative maxims and even the author too writes to teach the reader something in such a way that the entertainment value of his text and the educative value of it is balanced and harmonious. The author weaves values in his text in such a way that the reader is able to grasp those values to follow and lead a life worth living. When we say that the worth of a literary work is weight in gold, we mean that it is invaluable as it imparts life-values. The work of Shakespeare is still read and appreciated as it teaches us how to lead a purposeful life. Tulsidas is read because he teaches us the value that is *dharma*. The study of a literary work as a means for moral education is a long established practice as it has the power to imbibe in us the values and morals that have survived the day. As fantasy writer Brandon Sanderson puts it, 'All stories have been told before. We tell them to ourselves, as did all men who ever were. And all men who ever were will be. The only things new are the names.'[19] When our great Rashtrkavi Maithili Sharan Gupt equates literature with the over-powering sun, in the tradition of where the sun cannot reach the poet will, he is keeping in view the inspiring value-based meaningful literature.

अंधकार है वहाँ, जहाँ आदित्य नहीं है।
मुर्दा है वह देश, जहाँ साहित्य नहीं है।

(Darkness is there, where there is no sun.
Death is there, where there is no literature.)

Similarly Dr. Nishank tells us the stories of his surroundings laced with virtues and vices, hidden and presented as characters. In his poems we find him following the great universal values in spite of admitting the loss of these values around us. He is also of the view that in today's world, life-values and poetry are poles apart (see the preface of his selected poetry, especially *aye vatan tere liye, samarpan, navankur, mujhe vidhata banana hai, desh ham jalne n denge, jeevan path mein and matr bhumi ke liye*) but the poet in Nishank is persistent in knitting the two. The fabric he so makes and we fondly may term as 'text' is fabulous. I say it after reading almost all his selected poems that he is hailing the muse only to get inspiration and give inspiration to live and die for the sake of the motherland. It is his value—proposition and scheme.

Long ago, inscribed on the forecourt of the Temple of Apollo at Delphi was the maxim, 'Know thyself.' Reading literature remains the surest means to do just that—to live the life. Socrates declared the only one worth living is the examined life. The reading of Nishank's text provides us examples of lives already examined and found worth emulating.

Dr. Nishank has already become popular and well-known today as a powerful creator of texts through his versatile talent articulated in prose and poetry. He has proven himself as a sensible sensitive poet, who has been spearheading a literary movement of national awakening. Through his novels and short stories, he has been very authentically and creatively representing his region Uttarakhand. Devbhumi Uttarakhand or God's own county is distinctly amazing and conspicuously singular. Her varied identity along with her wide-ranging social, economic, cultural, religious and geographical features are portrayed and woven so skilfully by the master-craftsman Nishank in his writings that he is being placed one among a few authors of his region. It doesn't mean that Dr. Nishank is a regional author. He writes on his region, but his range and span encompass his region, nation and reach the world. His perseverance and literary pursuit is not centred on the dictum 'art for art's sake'. He is here to write with a purpose, a solemn purpose and pledge he must have taken to rejuvenate and revitalise society at large.

There are Indians who see in Dr. Nishank a political leader from the so-called cow-belt. There are some who have heard that Dr. Nishank is a devout Hindi man. Those who have been ardent readers and followers of contemporary creative writing in Hindi are familiar with Dr. Nishank's writings. The reach of Dr. Nishank may be limited to the readers of Hindi at present, but a beginning has already made and one can find many of his books translated into French, German and English, etc. Some of his books are available in a number of Indian languages, such as Marathi, Telugu, etc. He has made solid connection with his readers. And the rest follows.

□

4

Poetic Merit Revisited

"Honest criticism and sensitive appreciation is directed not upon the poet, but upon the poetry."[1] —*T.S. Eliot*

We all know that language is all-pervading and we all love our language, but language is not literature. Words are not literature, books are not literature and poems are not poetry. A *poem is* a piece of writing that has features of both speech and song, whereas *poetry* is the art of creating these *poems*. *Poetry* is also used to refer to poems collectively or as a genre of literature. Poetry is a word from the Greek language; it means creation. There is a potter; he makes pots. He is adept in the art of pottery. Similarly, there is a poet, who makes poems. A poet is a person who creates poetry. He is adept in the art of poetry. Dr. Ramesh Pokhriyal 'Nishank' is an out and out poet. For him poetry comes as naturally as leaves to a tree. My perception of poetry as a lofty literary form with little mass appeal has perished for good after reading a few of Nishank's poems. His proclivity and penchant for poetry is hard to miss as his fiction is also laced with lilting prose. The variety of themes he covers displays how he develops his particular sense of perception and patriotism.

This book is an introduction, a brief introduction. Once Agyeya told us that 'the role of an introduction is to prepare the ground; the ground is 'ready' when one can walk on it without anxiety and forget about it. Now is the time for the reader to walk on and meet the poet."[2] Therefore, like an adept gardener, I will prepare the ground for you to play. You are at liberty to read Nishank's selection. There is no need to start from the beginning. You can take a bit or bite by bite. (Some books are to be tasted, others to be swallowed and a few to be chewed and digested.- Bacon). Before I introduce you to the poet under discussion, let me tell you something about poet and poetry in general and Hindi poetry, in particular. The kind of poet Dr. Nishank is and the way he communicates in verse should also be placed in proper perspective. Unless we see him in the company of the masters of Hindi poetry, we will not be able to see his remarkable footing.

In the beginning, there was a tussle between philosophy and poetry to take the place of pride and it was said that philosophy is far better than poetry. In the West, Plato says that poets are imitators of the world and therefore are far from the truth. They are thrice removed from reality. They corrupt the youth by inciting their passion. Aristotle, his disciple, defines poetry as a 'medium of imitation' that seeks to represent or duplicate life through character, emotion, or action. Plato had a great distrust with regard to poets and poetry. From the following excerpt of his book, *The Republic* we can see that he doesn't like the poets because they are far away from truth:

> *"The imitative poet implants an evil constitution for he indulges the irrational nature which has no discernment of greater and less, but thinks the same thing at one time great and at another time as small; he is a manufacturer of images and is very far removed from the truth."*[3]

There are many poets who are not sure about the capacities of their poetry. Sir Philip Sidney (1554-1586), addressing general objections to poetry such as those of Plato, declares that the purpose of poetry is 'to teach and delight'. Sidney's doctrine presents the poet as a creator. Similarly, William Wordsworth, in his 1802, *Preface to the Lyrical Ballad* uses the word 'pleasure' more than 50 times, proposing that the 'end of poetry is to produce excitement in coexistence with an overabundance of pleasure.' Bakhtin, the proponent of dialogism, was also of the opinion that poetry is 'authoritarian, dogmatic and conservative, sealing itself off from the influence of extra literary social dialects' (1998:287). Suvir Kaul says that poetry is not 'an exercise of inwardness'[4] while Philippe Lacoue-Labarthe says that 'a poem commemorates. Its experience is an experience of memory.'[5] Poet Wallace Stevens points out, 'all poetry is experimental poetry.'[6] He tells us that the reading of a poem should be an experience (like experiencing an act) and its writing must be all the more so. Emily Dickinson's playful remark to her mentor Thomas Higginson, "If I feel physically as if the top of my head were taken off, I know that is poetry,"[7] is also a tongue-in-the-cheek comment on the power of poetry.

When Nishank writes, he too is experiencing this act and experimenting with verse for his innate and intimate feelings for the nation. Verse is often a term of disparagement in the world of poetry and has been often used to dismiss the work of people who want to write poetry but don't know how. Verse, in this usage, means unsophisticated or poorly written poetry. When George Orwell describes Kipling as 'a good bad poet', he is indicating that there are a great many good bad poetry in English. A poet is a poet is a poet. Therefore, Dr. Nishank's poetry has to be seen in such a perspective. Better or worse, verse is no more than verse.

In the West, there has been a gradual place for poetry. Firstly, poetry was seen with suspicion, but slowly it was accepted and appreciated. In India, from the very beginning, we have been placing a poet on a very high pedestal. A poet has been considered a creator like Brahma. It has been said, "Where the sun can't reach, a poet can reach there." Writing poetry is the fruit of good *karma* and so on. For Indians, literature and poetry have not been the two sides of the same coin; they are the coin itself. These two words have been synonymous. Indian critical tradition (*Kavyashastra)* takes us towards this direction. The basic theories in Indian aesthetics are those of *dhvani, rasa, alankara, vakrokti, riti* and *aucitya—rasalankrti vakrokti dhvani aucitikrama sahitya sastra etasmin sampradaya iti smrta.* Indians rely on *'rasa'* and the way of expression. Indian poetry has one *sutra* (rule) to define poetry as a work of art which is artistic only when it evokes the experience of *rasa*. According to Edward C. Dimock, Indian poetics may be appropriated for Indian literature. He believes that 'Sanskrit critics have taxonomic approach to the psychology of emotions. The 'taxonomic' involves more from the 'personal' to 'transpersonal'.[8] From Bharat Muni (*Natyashastra*) to Panditraj Jagannath (*Ras Gangadhar*) the tradition of writing books on poetics continued for no less than two thousand years. Later *kavi-shiksha* became a part of informal learning about Indian poetics. According to Rajshekhar, the poet is possessed of *karyitri pratibha* (creative faculty) and the reader is possessed of *bhavyitri pratibha* (appreciative faculty). A great poet possesses both the faculties. Dandin, the great critic, says that there are three causes of poetry: *naisargiki pratibha* (inborn talent), *nirmanla shastrgyan* (clear understanding of the texts) and *amanda abhiyoga* (constant application of the above-said genius). *Shakti* (inborn power), *vuyatpatti* (an accomplishment of knowledge of scriptures and literary taste) and *abhayas* (constant practice) are the requirements for a poet. The body of poetry, Dandin says, is a group of sounds which indicates the joyful aim (*istarth*) intended by the author. 'We have read poetry and we have heard poetry' should be followed by sentences as 'we have understood poetry and we have appreciated poetry'. When critic Vishvnath says that a sentence with *rasa* and Panditraj Jagannath says that it is a word promoting delight, the reader and the listener are apt to read or listen to it to get that delight and *rasa*.

Hindi Poetry

The poet writes for his age first and is greatly inspired by his age. Once upon a time, Hindi poets wrote to please the kings and their supporters. It was also considered proper to please the present and the future poets (आगे के कवि रीझें

तु कविताई) and if they couldn't let the poetry be considered as *bhakti* (devotion). Some poets, such as Bhushan, took up the lives of the living legend, like Shivaji, as a subject and by using hyperbolic language, they wrote poetry to let the entire locality and region reverberate with national pride.

During the 19th and early 20th centuries, because of the interference of foreign powers in India, poets started reacting in a different manner. They started giving preference to social and economic issues. The political struggle was in the background and the poets were busy in revitalising our glorious past also. Before Independence, poets, writing in English, such as Henry Louis Vivian Derozio (1809-1831) asked, "Why is it that literature doesn't flourish in this country?" The next generation of poets, such as Bharatendu Harishchandra (1850-1885), started answering the question by speaking about *Bharat durdasha* due to *angrez raj*. Tagore (1861-1941) was also of the view that the real problem in India was not only political, but also social. In the 19th century, poets turned to the nation as a deity and wrote poems to arouse passions of patriotism. Bharatendu called it *desh vatsalta* (love for the country). Maithili Sharan Gupt (1886-1964) termed the countrymen as *desh vatsal*. During our freedom movement, poets were of the view that a noble character like Rama was just enough to be a reasonably good poet. Poets and scholars had to make concentrated effort to instil in us the feeling of bravery and patriotism. Maithili Sharan Gupt (1886-1964) wrote *Bharat Bharati*, a work full of patriotic feelings. Jaishankar Prasad (1889-1937) wrote '*Arun yah madhumay desh hamara*'. His poem *Beeti Vibhavari* gave the message of awakening to his fellow-countrymen. Suryakant Tripathi 'Nirala' (1896-1961) urged Indians to wake up from their age-old slumber in the poem, *Jago fir Ek Baar*. Makhan Lal Chaturvedi (1889-1968) wrote *Pushp ki Abhilasha* and Subhadra Kumari Chauhan (1904-1948) penned *Khub Ladi Mardani'*. Ramdhari Singh 'Dinkar' (1908-1974) addressed India and her people. Poems, such as *Mere Nagapati Mere Vishal* gave him a place of pride among Hindi nationalist poets. When Allama Iqbal (1877-1938) wrote his poem *Himala* in Wordsworthian grand style, his nationalism was at par with anyone.

इम्तिहान-ए-दीदा-ए-जाहिर में कोहिस्ता है तू
पासबाँ अपना है तू दीवार-हिंदुस्ताँ है तू।[9]

(To an outward sight you are a mountain range
For us, you are our guard, the wall of Hindustan.)

You can very well compare it with *Mere Nagpati Mere Vishal* of Ramdhari Singh 'Dinkar'.

मेरे नगपति! मेरे विशाल! साकार दिव्य गौरव विराट,
पौरुष के पुंजीभूत ज्वाल! मेरी जननी के हिम-किरीट![10]

Unlike previous erotic Braj-*bhasha* poets, the khadi-boli Hindi poets have been very careful about their mission. Babu Syam Sundar Das (1875-1945) has described the ultimate mission of *khadi-boli* Hindi Poetry as follows:

उसका काम है—पथ-भ्रष्ट को मार्ग बतलाना, आलसी में उत्साह भरना, पद-दलित को पूर्व सुनाना और मुर्दे को जिंदा करना।[11]
(Its very purpose is to guide on to the right path all those who are lost, to fill the lethargic with energy, to tell those who are ground under tales of past glory and so bring the dead back to life.)

There were several poets, well-known, lesser-known and unknown, who had been writing for the masses. They had been writing to accomplish the task given to them. They were Hindi-*sevi* and poetry for them was simply a medium of serving the nation. For instance, the Hindu *aarti*, '*Om jai Jagdish hare*' is here, there and everywhere but its creator, Shraddha Ram Phillouri (1837-1881) never got the due credit for it. The school prayer, *Vahsahkti hamen do dayanidhe,* is everywhere but the poet Murari Lal Sharma 'Balbandhu' (1883-1961) remained relatively unknown. A large number of poets remain unknown because the readers are more concerned about the product and not the person who created it. When India became free and was declared a republic, poets started underlining the theme of India as narrated in our national anthem and in books, such as *Discovery of India*. Those poets who sang the song *Vande matram* turned to issues India had at that point of time. The poets started turning their gaze towards the offspring of Mother India. On the one hand, the days of distress were over and happiness was all around, on the other, the poets understood the sad state of affairs in social and economic life and continued attracting the audience for the sake of oneness among the people of India. That is why when poets write on contemporary India, they not only write about *desh* (nation) and *desh bhakti* (devotion to the nation), they write about the real state of affairs. The first history of Hindi literature (1929) was written by Ramchandra Shukla (1884-1941) and was also revised by him way before Independence. After 1947, many scholars tried their hands in this area but the most arresting one was by Acharya Ram Swarup Chaturvedi (1931-2003). In the lines that follow, he hints at the main parameter with which one can identify a great poet:

> बड़े कवि की एक पहचान यह हो सकती है कि कविता उसने अपने युग की संवेदना से बनाई है या नहीं।···आज के कवि के सामने राष्ट्रीयता का एक सीमित पक्ष, राजनीति के रूप में बहुत कठोर कच्चा माल है, जिससे कविता बनाना कवि-कर्म के लिए निश्चय ही बड़ी चुनौती है।[12]
>
> (One of the characteristics of a great poet can be whether he has woven his poetry with the texture and feel of his time or not. Before a contemporary poet, a very limited side of nationality is revealed and he has a very hard raw material to make use of. That is why it is a great challenge for the poet's profession to write nationalistic poetry.)

He is of the view that a poem is an extension of the meaning of life and criticism is the extension of that meaning. Therefore, it is to be understood that to understand poetry, the critic has to understand the poetry and shouldn't look to it through the eye of a system of thought, ideology or ism.

If you wish to 'take a stroll in the landscape of Hindi verse', you have a starting point somewhere in the early 20th century. This was the time when *khadi boli* or standard Hindi showed a definite direction towards self-realisation. There is no point discussing here the golden age of Hindi poetry—*bhakti kaal*—as we want to place the contemporary poet, Dr. Ramesh Pokhriyal 'Nishank', in the firmament of modern Hindi poets. The poets of Dwivedi era (1900-1918) in modern Hindi literature and who were largely inspired by Acharya Mahair Prasad Dwivedi (1864-1938) through the iconic magazine *Saraswati*, wrote poetry with national aspirations to hold their heads high. Mahavir Prasad Dwivedi encouraged the young and budding poets of his time to write poems in *khadi boli* (modern Hindi and not Braj *bhasha*). He also gave them directions to write on subjects, such as national pride and social reform. Maithili Sharan Gupt, Ayodhya Singh Upadhaya 'Hairoudh', Shridhar Pathak, Ramnaresh Tripathi, Narthuram Sharma 'Shankar', Gaya Prasad Shukla 'Sanehi', Satyanarayan 'Kaviratn', Gopal Sharan Singh, Siyaram Sharan Gupt and several others wrote poems underlining Indian values and ideals and tried their best to awaken the masses in their struggle for freedom from the British yoke. Maithili Sharan Gupt, just to name one, wrote *Bharat Bharati* to awaken Indians and to rekindle in them the love for their past glorious history. The poem *Bharat Bharati* has 'perhaps little poetic quality', says McGregor ;and should be seen for the use of verse in social and political discussion.' The point to keep in mind is that the poets who had been taking up such subjects and issues generally cared for 'what to say' and not 'how to say it' in an embellished language.[13] Later Subhadra Kumari Chauhan, Makhan Lal Chaturvedi, Sohan Lal Dwivedi, Bal Krishna Sharma 'Naveen' and others joined in the lead. Harivansh Rai Bachchan, Bhagvati Charan Varma, Narendra Sharma, Rameshvar Shukla 'Anchal',

Gopal Singh Nepali also joined this movement. Though the first four prominent *chayayvadi*—Nirala, Pant, Prasad and Mahadevi were mainly writing the sensuous description of the geographical landscape and their own personal feelings, like the great English Romantic poets, such as Wordsworth, Shelley and Keats, yet they too couldn't remain fully detached from the reality of life in British colonial India and hereafter. They were not locked in their own ivory towers and the undercurrent of nationalism was all-pervading in their work.

The Communist Party of India was founded in 1925 and a large number of writers and poets looked at Marx and his work with curiosity. *Pragativad* in Hindi literature soon followed. In fact, in 1836, Premchand very eloquently spoke on *The Nature and Purpose of Literature* at the first conference of Progressive Writers' Association. *Pragativad—pragati*—is something in forward motion. The entire Hindi literary world got charmed by this movement, But it started showing a declining trend in the 1950s. In fact, when Agyeya, the poet, brought out a collection of *Taar Saptak* (meaning upper octave) in 1943, he underlined the need for experimental poetry because the earlier movements were failing in their task self-imposed by them. His *Pryogvad* (Experimentalism) which later got transformed into *Nai Kavita* was a new turn in Hindi poetry to get rid of *Pragativadi* propaganda. About this trend, German academic, Lothar Lutze, says with authority, "1943 marked the birth of Hindi literariness (*literaturetum*). *Prayogvad* was the first purely literary movement in Hindi poetry."[14] Agyeya was of the view that the experimental poets were not claiming that they had got the ultimate truth of poetry, but they could very well claim that they were the 'seekers'. Even though *Nai Kavita* and a number of movements and strands cropped up in Hindi poetry, the overall scenario remained blurred with critics and scholars claiming different things at different times.

The quest of the ideal man failed miserably after India got her Independence. The love for motherland turned upside down. The idea of 'little man' (*laghu manav*) brought forward by *Nai Kavita* directed the poets to sing songs of the ordinary man. No ideal, idea and ideology could guide and instruct the poet. The poets remained 'unchained' and 'free'. They abandoned old prosodic features and figures of speech and experimented with the rhythm of meaning. Jagadish Gupt wrote in detail about *arth kee laya* (rhythm of meaning) following Eliot's and Richard's ideas about symbiosis of meaning and rhythm. In the West, Richards was very much in favour of 'rhythm of the mental activity through which we apprehend not only the sounds of the words, but their sense.' In Hindi, the new poets generously started using it.

The change of prosody from alliterative lines to prose-like sayings is still in vogue. The contemporary poet is not against it. As far as the subject of poetry is concerned, the poets are still presenting poems in which the strand of nationalism is both hidden and apparent. India, Hindustan, Bharatmata, *deshbhakti* and *deshprem* are all-pervading. Kumar Visvas and Hari Om Pawar, both became famous by reciting their patriotic poems. In the age of social media, humour and nationalism are more in demand than other themes. The overriding change, though perceived by critics in terms of the manner of putting the words on paper, is palpable but the inherent theme is still nationalistic and people-centric. Akshaya Kumar says:

> *"From the high-pitched Sanskritic nationalism of pre-Independence, Hindi poetic imagination thus veers towards subaltern nationalism, negotiating in the process the demands as well as anxieties of statism. It unleashes different configurations of nationalism as much as it is animated by them. If in pre-Independence Hindi poetry, the endeavour is to work out a duplicitous poetics of nationalism (of resistance and collaboration), in the post-Independence phase, the self-critical poets question the politics of forging such an ambivalent form of nationalism. The people-centric imperatives, operating for a while under the pressures of high nationalism, come forth in the open as its quasi-spiritual illusions*

fail to lull them into obedience. Hindi poetry takes an ideological turn from a statist position, moving towards the societal one. Nationalism, and finally, people-centric socialism are thus the three stepping stones in the broad evolutionary trajectory of Hindi poetic imagination."[15]

This is the background or the platform where one can place Dr. Nishank. We have been instructed by our elders that we must have time to stand and look back, look around and then march forward. It's not advisable to jump the gun. Therefore, by way of recollection, the distance travelled so far is presented in a nutshell. I hope that it is going to be useful.

Nishank, the Poet

Dr. Yogendra Nath Sharma 'Arun', *'il miglior fabbro'*— I have used this title which means 'the better craftsman' for Dr. Arun, for obvious reasons. He has been Pablo Neruda for Dr. Nishank? In the foreword to an edited book, *Dr. Nishank ke Kavya mein Indradhanushi Chintan*, he says that Dr. Nishank must have been writing poetry because of his *karma* of the previous lives. I don't know much about the previous lives but I am enamoured and impressed with the lines quoted here. Dr. Arun begins the foreword of the book as follows:

> महाकवि जयशंकर प्रसाद ने कहा है कि 'कविता करना अनंत पुण्यों का फल है' अर्थात् कवि सचमुच अपने पूर्व जनमों के अनंत पुण्यों के फलस्वरूप ही काव्य का सृजन कर पाता है। डॉ. रमेश पोखरियाल 'निशंक' निस्संदेह माँ सरस्वती के ऐसे वरदपुत्र हैं, जिन्होने अनंत पुण्यों के फलस्वरूप प्राप्त कवित्व-प्रतिभा से हिंदी काव्य का भंडार भर दिया है।[16]
>
> (The great poet Jaishankar Prasad says that 'Writing poetry is a boon of doing so many good deeds.' It means a poet is able to write poetry as a result of his collected good *karmas* in reality. Without any doubt, Dr. Ramesh Pokhriyal 'Nishank' is such a great son of Mother Saraswati who has enriched the treasure of Hindi poetry with his poetic genius which he has received because of the countless great deeds done in his previous lives.)

The editor is extolling the poetic genius of Dr. Nishank as it is his editorial duty to do so. Dr. Arun is a poet and like most Hindi poets of his temperament and advanced age, he also is of the view that poetry is a divine blessing. On the other hand, critic and translator A.K. Ramanujan says that 'poems aren't even words/ enough to rankle, infect/ or make smallest incisions.'[17] Frances Wilson (1964-) says that poetry is a horrible waste of time. The scant regard for poetry by some critics notwithstanding, the poets, in general, are given very high regard by the Indian community. They are said to be the harbinger of good omen.

I would also like to add that to give full credit to the divine is to undermine the hard work; to put it in the words of T.S. Eliot, 'the intolerable wrestle with the word'. It takes a lot of inspiration and perspiration even to write a couplet. I would call it *sanskar* (upbringing). I will include the *sanskar* of the previous lives and add to it the *parishkar* of this life to make Nishank into a poet. It is in this sense that the word *sanskar* is used by Sumitra Nandan Pant (1900-1977) in his Introduction to the poetry collection *Pallav* (1926). In the introduction, Pant expresses dissatisfaction that Hindi speakers think in one language and express themselves in another. He feels that Braj *bhasha* is out of date and seeks help to usher in a new national language. Who can forget his definition of poetry given in the preface?

> कविता हमारे परिपूर्ण क्षणों की वाणी है।
> (Poetry is the language of our supreme moments.)

This definition should be compared with William Wordsworth's definition of poetry. This definition is so well known and oft-cited that it needs no citation:

> *"Poetry is the spontaneous overflow of powerful feelings: it takes its origin from emotion recollected in tranquillity."*

I see some distant relationship between these two poets—Pant and Nishank—both hailing from the same geographical region. Dr. Nishank has been enriching himself knowingly and unknowingly resulting into an active change of state without a drastic change of context. His literary *sanskar* must have either been given to him by his family or local traditions and tastes or is acquired through education or contact with the outer world. His experience in life –good and bad—must have given him a chance and challenge to speak up for those who can't. Like Kabir, he has neither read *pingal* (the art of prosody) nor tried to imitate others. The poetic impulse with the knowledge and understanding of the use of right words in the right order makes poetry worth reading. Dr. Nishank must have been using his own variety of Hindi (not *khadi boli/manak* Hindi) during his formative years. I assert that it was his acquired literary *sanskar* that came via formal education, through different contact-zones (a term used by Mary Louise Pratt to refer to social spaces where cultures meet, clash and grapple with each other), with the printed word and its numerous genres. No doubt it was the means of identifying with a wider community (both a provincial community and the imagined national one, as put forward by one of Dr. Nishank's translators, namely Dr. Chetana Pokhriyal in *The Seeds of Creation*.

Poet Nishank is not from the so-called *khadi-boli* region, like Muzaffarnagri Shamsher Bahadur Singh and Roorkeewale Dr. Yogendra Nath Sharma 'Arun'. Nishank is extra-territorial, like Agyeya and Muktibodh. He is from the region from where *chayavadi* Sumitra Nandan Pant arrives and it is the nature and magnanimity of the Hindi language that Nishank is also a Hindi poet like all of them. The difference is of time and tenor. It is to be said with conviction resulting from a careful reading of a number of Nishank's poems that here is a poet who requires no adjective or superficial superlatives, but urgently requires critical and careful reading and analysis. The appreciation will follow suit. Here is a poet who is transforming his life-experiences into poems that inspire. Here is a poet who has no desire to show off the capacity of his range. Dr. Nishank is not a poet of dictionary and glossary; he is a poet who doesn't speak for himself. He allows his words to do so.

Indeed it is surprising yet satisfying that Nishank as a poet could write countless poems and got more than a dozen selections of his poems published. It is also to be noted that his poems are translated frequently into English and other world languages and several Indian languages including Tamil, Telugu, Marathi, Kannada, Gujarati, and Punjabi. It is also worth noting that three book-length studies of various selections of his poetry, short stories and novels have recently been released and the research papers on these three books have been written by prominent names from the Hindi world. Ezra Pound once said that "great literature is simply language charged with meaning to the utmost possible degree." Similarly Dr. Hari Mohan, in an article published in one of the above-mentioned books, has this to say about Nishank the poet, in whom he finds 'simplicity' and 'life'. Dr. Mohan could say this after carefully looking at the personality and poetry of Dr. Nishank.

> सहजता कवि की सबसे बड़ी विशेषता है। यह उनके व्यक्तित्व से आती है। 'निशंक' जैसे सहज-सरल व्यक्ति हैं, उनकी कविताएँ भी वैसी ही सहज-सरल और सीधी हैं। कविताओं को पढ़कर लगता है कि ये मुक्ति, समर्पण, कर्म, और जीवन की कविताएँ हैं। उनकी कविताओं में जीवटता है और अलग राह बनाने की बेचैनी भी। लेकिन अलग एकाकी चलने की स्वार्थपरक नीति के वे प्रबल विरोधी हैं। वे सभी को साथ लेने की बात कहते हैं। वे आज के जीवन के संघर्षों, विडंबनाओं, द्वंदों को समझते हैं, इसीलिए आकाश की बात नहीं करते, धरती की बात करते हैं।[18]
>
> (Minimalism or utter simplicity is a remarkable feature of the poet. It comes from his personality which is devoid of any snobbery and unwanted sophistication. Like the person, his poems are also plain and simple, without any extravagance. The reader will take these verses as the voice of a man who is liberated and

dedicated towards his mission. The liveliness of his poems comes from his innate liveliness and the despair is just a passing phase in his joyous world. He is a poet of the masses and not the classes. Their pangs and pains are his, their joys and elation he weaves in his poems is theirs. He has nothing to hide and nothing to keep aside.)

It is said by many scholars that his range of poetic themes is not limited to patriotic fervour. It extends from patriotism to national unity, national integrity, public good and welfare, social awareness, political movements and activities, past glories and future hopes, present challenges and opportunities. Nishank, the poet, has a life-vision of his own which is crystal clear. In line with this vision, his expressions, his contemplation, move accordingly. There is the sharpness in his vision and ideological vitality. In his poetic statements and versification, he is not only socially and nationally agile but also has an innate sense of duty. He is not only undaunted in the wake of challenges and struggles but also these provide him inner strength, energy and motivation. His devotion for the motherland is expressed in stanzas as follows. Nishank's poetry at times is such that the reader forgets him and remembers his lines only to be used from time to time:

सैकड़ों मस्तक चढ़े माँ, मैं भी उनमें एक हूँ।
चाहता हूँ वंदनीय माँ, क्षण व कण प्रत्येक दूँ॥

(I am one of the hundreds of heads sacrificed
for the motherland.
I wish Reverend Mother to forfeit every moment
and spark of my life.)

Such poems can be seen as pertinent attempts to present our shared experiences. He is not so much writing for entertainment or delight as much as he writes to inspire and guide. In this way, his words are the arrows aimed at certain evils around us. He ventures deep into the wilderness of life in search of rocky and uneven passions. His poetry is the passionate expression of powerful feelings not expressed before in such a way. There is no point in searching the quality of these poems based on our pedantic poetic sensibility and university tutoring. His expressive poetry is like an innocent child, pure and simple, inornate and unadorned, but loveable and beyond words.

Nishank is not writing as a jilted lover or an outcast, full of anger. He has no ulterior motive, no ism to follow, no ideology to propagate. Hindi poetry is sometimes marred with Marxism, feminism and Dalitism and is read with the name of the poet attached with it. Keshavdas, Kabirdas and Tulsidas are all recognised by their writings. Some poets used to write just to please their powerful masters or astound their rivals. Nishank is free from all this. If you go through his voluminous work, you will find gems of beauty scattered all around. Very short poems are written by such great poets as Pablo Neruda too. Though there is no comparison whatsoever between them, yet a poem as follows will keep you surprised as if you are reading Pablo's poem *Always*(I am not jealous of what came before me.):

तुम्हारे सौदे
तुम्हारे सौदे भी
कुछ अजीब होते हैं
वे भी किसी-किसी का नसीब होते हैं
तुम बस एक छोटी सी मुस्कराहट
देते हो
और हमें
जिंदगी भर के लिए अपना बना लेते हो।[19]
(Dealings,
Your dealings are somewhat strange.
For only a few selected by fate
You just exchange an elfin smile
And enchain us for life.) (*My translation*)

Dr. Nishank considers these poems as they are. (ये क्षणिकाएँ जैसी हैं, बिल्कुल अपने जैसी हैं) । (These poems wish to capture a tiny moment in the basket of words. And what you read is words filled with emotions recollected in tranquillity and turmoil of this mundane life.)

In 1919, T.S. Eliot published an essay *Tradition and Individual Talent* in which he formulated his principle of relationship between a poet and his poetic and literary traditions. Reading Nishank as a poet, even this poem, reminds me of several other poems. The reader will also be able to associate the poet's intention with his/her experience. The reader of Hindi who has been fed the diet of poems, such as: *'Binu, moul hee bikane, man lehun to dehun chantak nahin'* will be able to connect well.

Poetry as Resistance

Some poets insist, as Langston Hughes writes, 'That all these walls oppression builds/will have to go!' Others seek ways to actively 'make peace', as Denise Levertov implores, suggesting that 'each act of living' might cultivate collective resistance. There are some others who write to inspire values—universal and local—instil confidence and use their pen for nation building. The different kinds of poetry have always been there. During the freedom struggle, it was there in *Jhansi kie Rani* and *Pushp ki Abhilasha* and after Independence, '*Sinhasan khali karo ki janta aati hai*". The political power of poetry is immense. During India's Emergency, anti-State poetry proliferated. Though anti-Emergency poetry did little to bring about the restoration of democracy yet poets, such as Atal Bihari Vajpayee wrote using a pen-name (*Kaidi Kavirai*) and were appreciated.

What is the purpose of writing resistance poetry if it is not meant to directly influence politics nor to be great art? When we study Nishank's poetry and find out a collection aptly titled *Sagharsh Jari Hai* (Resistance Continues), we are told that his poetry is entirely free (यह कविता परम स्वाधीन है—Dr. Sudha Rani

Pandey). What is so great about this statement? Muktibodh too said this about poetry as such:

नहीं होती, कहीं भी खत्म कविता नहीं होती परम स्वाधीन है।

This is the basic feature of poetry. Poetry must be eternally free. Actually freedom for poetry and freedom of poets are two different issues. As Nishank himself says:

शब्द कभी मरते नहीं हैं।

There is nothing new in this statement too. What is new is the self-realisation of the poet through his songs and poetry.

स्वयं को जाना है मैंने
गीत में
यह शब्द-रचना नहीं
मेरा चिर मीत है।
मेरा अस्तित्व है।[20]

(I atttained self-realisation
In songs.
This is not a collection of words
But my forever friend,
My very being...)

The resistance is there in some of Nishank's poems but without confrontation. If there is something, it is the search for insight within. He is there in the vortex of politics like the fabled Abhimanyu surrounded by the tumult of propaganda.

दुष्प्रचार की आँधी में भी निशंक अकेला खड़ा हुआ हूँ।
राजनीति के चक्रव्यूह में, अभिमन्यु-सा घिरा हुआ हूँ।।[21]

(Nishank stands alone even amidst the storm of propaganda
Like Abhimanyu surrounded by the rotund wheels of politics.)

Here you will appreciate that Nishank is not only a person or the poet of these lines but also a representative of the untrodden masses who tirelessly toil for freedom and dignity. Nishank becomes the embodiment of one who goes in for the sake of *dharma* and finds himself surrounded by deceitful persons whose sole aim is to grind their own axe and subvert the plans of those who mean business for the sake of common folk.

Poetry as Emotional Outburst

> We look before and after, and pine for what is not;
> Our sincerest laughter with some pain is fraught;
> Our sweetest songs are those that tell of saddest thought.[22]

Percy Bysshe Shelley, the Romantic poet and critic, has his distinct views about the role of 'imagination' and poetry. On the other hand, the other English poets of the Romantic Age and *Chayavaadi* Hindi poets, both considered poetry as emotional outbursts. The definition of poetry by Wordsworth and the couplets of Jaishankar Prasad indicate poetry as being a sort of emotional outburst. In the words of Wordsworth, "poetry has its origin in emotions recollected in tranquillity." In *Ansu*, Hindi poet Jaishankar Prasad says:

> जो घनीभूत पीड़ा थी मस्तक में स्मृति-सी छाई
> दुर्दिन में आँसू बनकर वह आज बरसने आई।[23]

> (It was pain, that demonic cloud,
> spread memory-like in the mind.
> Arrived to drench me as tears in my bad days...)

Pain is compared to a cloud. It is a psychological and emotional pain and I am tempted to associate it with the *shloka*, मा निषाद of Valmiki, who was instrumental in the advent of poetry from pain:

(Hunter, you wouldn't be able to attain solace (or glory)

Because you killed a bird when it was mating with its partner.)

In *Kamayani*, Prasad's magnum opus, philosophy overpowers poetry. But in *Ansu* philosophy is subdued and poetry shines. Poetry is considered an emotional outburst in pain. It is repeatedly said by John Keats who had been writing on overcoming pain and Harivansh Rai Bachchan (for example, *nisha nimantran*—The call of the Night), who wrote poems surrounded by unseen but thoughtful solitude. It describes every painful moment, from dusk to dawn, of lonely nights spent without rest. This is poetry at its best. In the age of *Chayavaad*, Bachchan could write poetry as *jeevanvaad* (the poetry of life). Dr. Nishank's poetry is also filled with the same kind of *jeevan-hala*, which is synonymous with the elixir of life. Even tears here are for gaining life.

क्रांति पर्व है आज उधर, कौन यहाँ दु:ख शांत करेगा?
सूर्य-किरण सा कब सुत मेरा, देहरी पर आलोक भरेगा।।[24]

(Today there is celebration-time, who will pacify us here?
When would my sun-bright son, enlighten the doorsteps?)

Now, you can very well understand why I invoked so many poets from the East and the West. It was to prove a point that Dr. Nishank, as a poet, is a poet of tender emotions also. He writes about a widowed mother who has been waiting for her son's return but he doesn't come as he is in the service of his motherland. This is in the league of those poets I just mentioned. The complete helplessness of the mother on the one hand and her pining for her son's return is so poetically conveyed that the reader feels awe-struck, amazed and a little sullen.

चला गया जो, किंतु अभी भी, बाट जोहती माता।
वृद्धा देख रही निज सुत को, है गिरि पथ पर आता।।
खुली हुई हैं आँखें उसकी, किसी प्रतीक्षा में?
उड़ता उसका प्राण-पखेरू किस की अन्वीक्षा में?[25]

(One who went away, still awaited by her mother
Mother gazing for her son, homecoming crossing the hilly terrain
Fringed curtains of her eyes wide open, waiting for what?
Helpless soul fluttering to leave, reflecting for whom?)

In one stroke of the pen, the poet Nishank has travelled the entire gamut of creative impulse and the way it is taken by the reader is beyond words. The reader is transported into the realm of fancy and at the same time can't leave the untrodden terrain of real life in which waiting is the *karma* and *dharma* of an ordinary mortal. The entire poem, which is divided into four cantos, is an instance of poetic genius. If you are an avid reader of poetry, you will recollect Robert Frost's poem *Waiting* when you read this poem of epic length.

But on the memory of one absent, most,
For whom these lines when they shall greet her eye.[26]

The collective unconsciousness of mankind, Carl Jung highlights, the mother figure is one of the basic archetypes. Dr. Nishank takes an ordinary mother from an unknown hilly place and weaves a narration through his poetic genius in which the poem becomes a kind of longing, not only between the mother and her son, but also between the Almighty and the soul. The foregoing examples are sufficient testimony to the skill and variety of Nishank's poetic diction. It seems Nishank has also mastered this *anand chand*.

After reading *Pratiksha* through and through, one can well understand that the underlying meaning of the poem and its particular references are subject to various interpretations. The poet Nishank in his eagerness to help the reader gives a footnote where he writes:

अन्वीक्षा : दार्शनिक तत्त्वों (आत्मा-परमात्मा, जीव-जगत्, ब्रह्म-माया) आदि के चिंतन को अन्वीक्षा कहते हैं।[27]

> (The contemplation of philosophical elements (soul-divine, creature-cosmos, and *brahma-maya*) is called exploration (*anviksha*).]

It is apparent that at the surface level the poem is about an old mother and her son. Her longing for her son is the subject matter and can evoke a pensive feeling. She has a name and status and her son too is also a man in flesh and blood. I don't know for sure if the poet suggests or not—at least at times—as I am suggesting that the poem is an everlasting desire and longing for a meeting between the soul and the divine. Sheer beauty in the description of the mother as well as the hilly terrain is worth watching in almost all the couplets. Even the great devastating earthquake is mentioned. The day-to-day struggle to make both ends meet and the call of the motherland is balanced in such a way that the reader is in awe with the motive of the poet. The reader is over-awed when he reaches the last line in which the poet is in the line of the great *rashtrkavi* Maithlisharan Gupt and evokes the oft-quoted '*abla-sabla*' (destitute-prosperous) adjectives very commonly used for women in India.

A feminist reading of this book and for that matter a feminist reading of Dr. Nishank's work is highly desirable. Finally, a post-structuralist or deconstructive reading of *Pratiksha* might, in addition to these concerns, trace some other meanings. It is the mastery of the master-reader who, in the role of the reader, will read it according to his/her taste and understanding. A few may say that the story is still incomplete and the poet can very well add a few more lines to let the two meet for a happy ending. The text can be remade by the poet and the reader, both at will. This is the beauty and success of *Pratiksha*.

This is about one of his *khand-kavyas*. His stray poems are in thousands. Agyeya admits in the foreword of *Choutha Saptak* that the poems at present speak more and tell less. Nishank's poetry is just opposite to this. His poems tell more and speak less. If brevity is the soul of wit, the witticism can be seen in poems such as these.

दिन भर निठल्ले रहकर
हम बहुत व्यस्त हैं कहकर
आदर्श का चोला औढ़े
ये कथित आदर्शवादी
बात करते हैं,
किंतु
व्यर्थ का दंभ भरनेवाले
ये चाटुकार हैं, जो
नवनिर्माण से डरते हैं।[28]

(Idling the whole day
Pretending to be busy
These so-called idealists
Talk incessantly
But
Vain and proud these fellows
Are flatterers, who
Are afraid of making it new.)

The Poet-Politician Nishank

"Just as dawn announces sunrise, the birth of such people (leaders) announces the future rise of the nation. It is they, who first dream in their minds the edifice of the nation and drawing a picture of that edifice, they display it in front of the general public (sarvasadharan) with speeches and articles. And through their speeches and articles, they forge whatever elements and strengths are needed to build that edifice."[29] *—Madan Mohan Malaviya*

The year Ramesh Pokhriyal was born in a nondescript village in the Himalayas, a poet-politician was lecturing on 'The Poet and the Politician'. He was Salvatore Quasimodo from Italy. He was awarded the Nobel Prize in Literature in

1959 "for his lyrical poetry which, with classical fire, expresses the tragic experience of life in our own times." The poet from Italy asked a pertinent question, "Can a poet and politician co-operate?" and replied in his Noble lecture, "perhaps they could in societies that are yet not fully developed." Long back, Plato propounded his views on the poet's function in an ideal republic and during the Romantic age, P.B. Shelley called the poets as 'unacknowledged legislators'. It is still debated if they could live in harmony. It is still not settled if a poet and a politician can live in the same body and soul.

Francesca Orsini in her path-breaking research on *The Hindi Public Sphere* (2006) starts a chapter on the Hindi politician. She says that politicians like Madan Mohan Malaviya and Purushottam Das Tandon established Hindi as a legitimate language of political exchange and the language of *swarajya*. Yes, there have been many politicians who used Hindi as an instrument of pride and solidarity. There have been others who are basically poets and writers but became politicians. Their numbers differ but they are still found around us. Whether Babu Sampurnanand and Seth Govinddas were basically politicians or writers can't be said with conviction. On the other hand, Maithili Sharan Gupt and Ramdhari Singh 'Dinkar' were poets first and foremost. Where should we place Dr. Nishank in this company? Is he an author by accident and a politician by choice or visa-versa? Let us discuss and find out.

There have been scores of politicians who have been poets and writers. Some even excelled in their field. Winston Churchill won the Nobel Prize for literature. Barack Obama too writes poetry. When Obama was a 19-year-old student at Occidental College, he published two poems in the spring 1982 issue of *Feast*, the school's literary magazine. Leaders, including Abraham Lincoln, Mahatma Gandhi, and Martin Luther King Jr. were always friendly with literary stalwarts. They used their literary resources to expand their concerns for others and still teach a large section of society the finer lessons of amity between people of different faiths and races.

Tagore and Premchand and several others were in their own literary ways tried to awaken the society struggling to end the British rule and eradicate several social evils, including poverty and untouchabilty. There are scores of poet-politicians in several languages of our own. Subhadra Kumari Chauhan and Sarojini Naidu, both were active politicians. Atal Bihari Vajpayee was one among them and Narendra Modi too wrote poems in Gujarati and Hindi. Ramesh Pokhrial 'Nishank' is also one among their ilk. I argue that Ramesh Pokhariyal 'Nishank' got greatly inspired by Atal Bihari Vajpayee and has been following Atalji's advice to this day—"You stop anything but never stop writing."

> *"You stop anything but never stop writing" were the words of advice of former Prime Minister Atal Bihari Vajpayee to BJP MP-and-author Ramesh Pokhriyal 'Nishank'. Speaking to reporters after presenting to President Pranab Mukherjee the first copy of a book, he has authored on the life of Vajpayee, Pokhriyal said, "Whenever I met him (Vajpayee), the first thing he used to ask is whether you are writing or not?" Stop anything but never stop writing."*[30]

Let me start with Atal Bihari Vajpayee who has been a mentor of the poet-and-politician Ramesh Pokhriyal 'Nishank'. Both of them can be compared well. It is more than a coincident that both have a pen-name. Atal ji used to write as '*Kaidi Kavirai'* and Ramesh Pokhriyal is 'Nishank" for all. Both had a background of print journalism. Atal's patriotic poetry is meant first and foremost to ignite the readers and the listeners and activate their latent talent for the service of the country. In his youth, during the freedom movement, Atal Bihar Vajpayee wrote poems on Bharat Mata, etc. His later poems mostly revolve on the fleeting nature of life, the insubstantiality of human achievement and on his sense of weariness. He used to say, "Had I not become a politician, I would have become a leading Hindi poet. I don't know about that, but there is no doubt in my mind that politics did interfere with my evolution as a poet."[31] He was always concerned about his position as a politician. In one of his poems, Atal Bihari Vajpayee says:

मेरे प्रभु!
मुझे इतनी ऊँचाई कभी मत देना,
गैरों को गले न लगा सकूँ,
इतनी रुखाई कभी मत देना।[32]
(My Lord!
Never bestow upon me such height
that I cannot embrace a stranger,
Never put me in such insensitive plight.")

Atal's poems, written in jail during the Emergency, tell us the poignant tale of those difficult times. "These are poems written by a man capable of reflection, who has not measured up to his own expectations. It is as though something is on the tip of his tongue, which he has chosen never to let slip. And so, though they glisten with flashes of insight, his poems give nothing away about the Faustian nature of his climb to the heights,"[33] says Vasantha Surya.

It will be worthwhile to add here that the book written in 2006 by Dr. Nishank on Atal Bihari Vajpayee mentions many interactions between the two poet-politicians. I am tempted to quote the following extract from the book. Atal was speaking at a book release function for the release of a short story collection by Nishank. The above report notwithstanding, what he himself said and Dr. Nishank quoted in his book is also worth pondering with a view to understanding the relationship between politics and literature.

> राजनीति और साहित्य थोड़ी दूर तक साथ चलते हैं और फिर अलग हो जाते हैं और अलग भी इस तरह होते हैं कि उन पर राजनीति हावी हो जाती है और साहित्य की चर्चा मात्र होती है। साहित्यकार का और राजनीति के विद्यार्थी का संबंध रहना चाहिए। लेखन एक साधना है। अगर भावों को शब्दों में उतारा गया है तो समझना चाहिए उसमें मूल रूप है। ठोस

रूप लिया है। कुछ आकार चाहता है। आगे की यात्रा आगे शुरू होती है। निशंकजी निरंतर लगातार लिखते रहें यह मेरी कामना है। हम पढ़ते रहें यह हमारी इच्छा है।[34]

Hindi poetry and contemporary Indian politics continue together for a short distance before disengaging. Presently, we find no poet of eminence in the Rajya Sabha. People think that politics is active, rough and comparable to a war while poetry is passive, smooth and abstract. Our Prime Minister Shri Narendra Modi wrote some poems once and he is fond of citing a poem or two during parliamentary debates just as a means of verbal persuasion. But it is just a matter of luck that a poet-politician like Dr. Nishank sits in the Parliament as a cabinet minister. W.H. Auden says that poetic imagination is not at all a desirable quality in a statesman. A poet may do very well as a guerrilla fighter or a spy, but it is unlikely that he will be a remarkable member of a parliamentary committee (बारह बरस दिल्ली रहे और भाड़ ही झोंका किए—मैथिलीशरण गुप्त) Do you know, West Bengal's Chief Minister has written 63 books? In other words, poet-politicians seldom set the literary world on fire. They just happen to be there. But Dr. Ramesh Pokhriyal 'Nishank' seems to be in different league. Adrija Bose (Huffpost) finds in him 'the most poetic politician' so far. Dr. Nishank as a poet-politician in the league of 'वज्रादपि कठोराणि मृदुनि कुसुमादपि' who is not only able to balance but also harmonises the two sides of his persona and vocation.

Dr. Nishank as a Poet of Abundance

Dr. Nishank as a poet is a poet of abundance. His prolific writing is awe-inspiring. Kritika Sharma says, "The sheer volume of Nishank's work—44 books—would put him in the company of a giant of Hindi literature, like Munshi Premchand."[35] Some professors of Hindi who don't want to be identified say many things about him, though they have hardly read him. But those who read him find in his work the charm of belongingness and the seasoned uprightness. His work gives the idea of an India that is free from rotten isms and ifs. His poetry is not the poetry of the classes but is of the masses or the common men who read him. For him life is not a tale told by an idiot signifying nothing, as it is for William Shakespeare. Nishank has a knack of telling wonderful tales of life as lived by him to the fullest. Just for instance, a poem from *Srijan ke Beej* tells us to do everything required (*sab kar dalo*) as life begins and ends in tears. The great poet Tennyson indicates in one of his well-known poems "Tears, idle tears, I know not what they mean", whereas Nishank says that though life begins and ends in tears, yet one has an option to live life to the fullest by doing everything possible. In fact, in such poems, the poet seems to me to be following Tennyson's *Ulysses* ('I will drink life to the lees') in letter and spirit. In another poem he says:

बहुत ही नजदीक मेरे रह रही है जिंदगी
मैं अनोखी दास्ताँ हूँ कह रही है जिंदगी।[36]

(Life that lives very close to me says to me very often
I am an unusual tale to tell)

Such lines tempt me to pronounce that his poetry is largely for the people, and of the people who have travelled far and wide in the terrain called life. This is no poetry associated with the nawabs and the elite. It may even be called by them mediocre and trite. It may not suit the sophisticated, but it is for those who wish to be a poet but can't. It is the poetry of self-help and courage in the vissicitudes of life. He is not only an admirer of poets, such as Harivansh Rai Bachchan and Gopal Das 'Neeraj', but also is a follower of their charm in more ways than one.

पूछो जरा इन सपनों से, क्यों चले आते हैं।
कहाँ से ये आते हैं, कहाँ चले जाते हैं॥[37]

(Ask these dreams for a while
Why these dreams for a while
And where do they come from and disappear?)

There is a Hindi poem *Koshish karne Walon ki Haar nahin Hoti*. It is truly inspirational. People who persist, never fail. In Sanskrit, there is a saying, *Prayatnovidheyah*. The idea is grand. The poem is actually written by Shri Sohan Lal Dwivedi but more often than not, it is attributed to Dr. Harivansh Rai Bachchan. It is often said that the poem that inspires goes miles. The job of a social reformer, a politician and leader is also to teach and entertain. The poet is also a teacher who says that you have to light the lamp in such a way that it doesn't flicker and go off even in the face of adversity. Those who decide and are determined, they can bring Heaven on the Earth. The solemn pledge once taken can keep the spirits high. The job of a poet is to collect wisdom and present in such a way that pleases all.

> तूफान आने पर भी बुझे न
> तू दिया आज ऐसा जलाना
> संकल्प लेकर बढ़ो तो सही
> कोई मुश्किल नहीं स्वर्ग धरती पर पाना।[38]
> (Never go off even in tempest
> Light such a lamp now
> March forward with determination
> And bring heaven on earth with ease.)

You may find the above stanza devoid of any poetic quality and might reject such attempts as mere versification. There may be some merit in your assertion. I needn't say anything from my side and just reproduce the following for your perusal:

> जब भी कोई रचनाकार अपनी सृजन-यात्रा के प्रारंभिक चरण में होता है, उन दिनों उसके मन में उत्साह तथा जुनून का सागर हिलोरे ले रहा होता है, यही कारण है कि प्रत्येक रचनाकार की प्रारंभिक रचनाएँ कलात्मक शिल्प-सौष्ठव की कसौटी पर पूरी तरह से खरी न उतरते हुए भी चिंतन की प्रखरता तथा विद्रोही तेवर अपने में समाए रखती है।[39]
> (Whenever a poet is in the initial phase of his poetic journey, his heart is filled with a sea of passion,

enthusiasm and excitement. That is the reason the initial poems may not be artistically and figuratively free from slips but they are filled with the intensity and rebellious attitude of the poet.)

The poet has decided to use literature not only as a means of expression but also as a medium of social welfare and well-being for the people. Literature for him is to express the pains and sorrows of the common man.

मैंने वेदना को अपने गीतों में गुनगुनाया
इसके सुरों को अपनी आवाज है बनाया
रिमझिम ये सावन है, मेरे पास मेरा मन है
अनमोल ये रत्न है।[40]
(I whispered pain through my songs
Turned them over through my lofty voice
This rain lets my heart in leaps and bounds
Invaluable jewels for me to sustain forever.)

Let me put this into a perspective. I got a couple of lines of Nishank which sound very similar to the great poets of Hindi language. Rahim and Kabir are two poets who never claimed that they were trying to impress others with their poetry. They had a very modest but lofty aim. Kabir wanted to educate and guide his readers or listeners. Rahim also guided by a similar goal. Rahim is different from Kabir. Kabirdas is a great poet, though he is said to be unlettered and a little bit outspoken and rash. Rahim (1556-1627) is more erudite and intellectually stimulated. His poetry is as humble as a 'needle', not as pungent and aggressive as a 'sword'.

रहिमन देखि बड़ेन को, लघु न दीजे डारि।
जहाँ काम आवै सुई, कहा करै तरवारि।।

(Never discard lowly, for the sake of high;
Sword of little use where a needle works.)

देन हार कोई और है, भेजत जो दिन रैन।
लोग भरम हम पर करे, तासो नीचे नैन॥

(The giver is someone else, giving day and night.
But the world gives me the credit, so I lower my eyes.)

And here is Ramesh Pokhriyal 'Nishank' in *Parmatma*:

बहे गंगा के सम पावन, न बातों में बनावट हो,
न मुझ में हो छलावा और, न चेहरे पर दिखावट हो,
कहीं अनजाने में हो गलती, तो मुझे माफ कर देना
अहं ना हो।[40]

(Let me be as pure as the holy Ganga
No make-believe in conversation
No deceit in action, no pretence on face
If unknowingly I make a mistake, excuse me
My ego alas!) (*translation mine*)

The same humbleness, the same zeal and enthusiasm for the rustic and the oppressed that you may have observed in Abdul Rahim Khankhna Rahim, you will find in Ramesh Pokhriyal Nishank's poetic narration. Literariness comes from the way a writer uses the language. 'What oft was thought but never so well-expressed...' A text works by the emergence of emotive meaning from its verbal structures to be called as literary and literature. His poetry is filled with such gems and jewels.

The poetic practice of Dr. Nishank goes on at a smooth pace. His poems have anguish for the common men and society. They are filled with agony, pain and distress at the wretched of the earth. Whenever he is filled with happiness and sorrow, joy and sadness, he takes up the pen and presents in the form of a poem. His acumen is inspired by the dictum of welfare for all. He has a keen desire to do something and that something turns out to be a piece of poem. Like George Bernard Shaw, H.L. Mencken also said once and it squarely fits here: "I write in order to attain that feeling of tension relieved and function achieved which a cow enjoys on giving milk.'

One of his selections of poetry has the following poem as a prologue. It very sincerely tells us the reason of his writing is the pang of expression:

पाठक गण!
आशा–निराशा के बीच जूझता
थपेड़े खाता रहा,
कभी छल–कपट
तो कभी स्वार्थांधता के साथ–साथ
असहिष्णुता से टकराता रहा।
मैंने शूलों को भी फूल समझ
हृदय से लगाया,
छिद–छिदकर लहूलुहान हुआ, पर
मेरे गीतों को लोगों ने जगाया,
कष्टों को झेलते–झेलते
असह्य पीड़ा, वेदना, दुःख और दर्द
मेरे अभिन्न अंग बन गए।
लोग चैन से सोते रहे
और मैं जिंदगी–मौत से लड़ता रहा,
तभी तो विषम परिस्थितियों में भी
जीता रहा।
और करता रहा संघर्ष।
संघर्ष सिर्फ संघर्ष के लिए नहीं।
और इन्हीं संघर्षों
आक्रोशजन्य विद्रोह
और चुनौती के प्रश्न उठा रहा है।
देश हम जलने न देंगे—कविता–संग्रह।[41]

(Dear readers I have been moving back and forth
Between hope and despair
Standing fast before treachery and deceit

Selfishness and intolerance sometimes
I embraced even thorns
Deeming them flowers
And was wounded badly, but
My songs awakened the masses
Enduring pain and hurt
Wound and ache, suffering and agony
All became my indelible parts.
People slept comfortably at ease
And I continued fighting with life and death
That's why I continued living even during difficult time
And continued my struggle non-stop.
Struggle not just for struggle's sake
But revolt born from rage
And these struggles and challenges, revolt and rage
Turn into poems—a selection of poetry.
(*Translated by Gopal Sharma*)

This is the preface of a book, an anthology of his patriotic poems *Desh Ham Jalne na dDnge* (2009) in line with his philosophy of life in which the tone is of togetherness. The literal meaning of the title is 'We shall not allow the country to burn in flames'. He is in the line of poets and sages who very often talk about national identity and pride. For instance, our sages said, "राष्ट्राय स्वाहा, इदं राष्ट्राय इदं न मम" (I give it to the nation, it's not mine). Prasun Joshi, another poet from Uttarakhand, also very often says,

"My motherland asks me
when will you repay my debts
my skies ask me
when will you follow your religion?"

In fact, as said earlier, the poets have often taken up as their national duty to call upon the youth to make even the ultimate sacrifice for the sake of their motherland.

Dr. Nishank is not an idle poetaster. His life and struggle has been in his poems. To make them poems, he has used the experiences of his life as bricks and mortar. He has seen others enjoying and merry-making when he was trying to make both ends met. He is lucky that he didn't pay a very heavy price for his vocation. He has been facing challenges but life has given him a lot also.

> तूफान गोद में बिठा, अंधकार को मिटा।
> सब बेड़ियों को तोड़कर, स्नेह–सूत्र जोड़कर
> मैं निशंक बढ़ रहा।[42]
> (Taking tumult in my stride, decimating darkness
> Breaking all shackles, bonding the love-knot
> I march ahead fearlessly!)

Experiencing Nishank's Poetry through English Translation

Dr. Nishank's stories, poems and other writings are slowly but surely being translated into several Indian languages, including English. If we also include the celluloid versions of his work, we are amazed at his diversity and range. There is no doubt that translation plays a crucial role in enhancing the reputation of an author. The quality of Dr. Nishank's translation notwithstanding, we read a translated text when we don't know the source language. Those who have heard about Dr. Nishank but are not familiar with the Hindi language can try the translated version of some of his books. But there is a rider. This is what our master poet and novelist Agyeya said about our own language and the other's language.

> न हम अपनी भाषा दूसरे से सीख सकते हैं, न दूसरों की भाषा में हम अपने को पहचान सकते हैं। अपनी भाषा सीख और अपने को पहचान कर फिर हमें दूसरों की भाषाएँ भी सीखनी चाहिए, उनका ज्ञान भी ग्रहण करना चाहिए। उसके सहारे अपना शोध भी करना चाहिए।[43]
>
> (We cannot learn our own language from others; nor can we recognise ourselves in the language of others. Having learnt our own language and recognised ourselves, we should certainly learn other languages

and seek the knowledge available through them, re-examine ourselves in their light.)

Needless to say, translation is a stop-gap arrangement. Poetry translations attract very few readers. Pierre Bourdieu says that poetry in translation is "the disinterested activity par excellence". Translation is both impossible and necessary in Derrida's vision. In *Freud's Legacy*, Derrida says: "...any signified whose signifier cannot vary nor let itself be translated into another signifier without a loss of meaning points to a proper name effect."[44] The proper name is that which cannot be translated. For Derrida, translation is none other than transformation, albeit a regulated one, because equivalence is virtually impossible. Indeed, translation is 'a notion of transformation of one language by another, of one text by another'. Robert Frost in *Conversations on the Craft of Poetry,* writes by way of defining poetry, "I like to say, guardedly, that I could define poetry this way: it is that which gets lost out of both prose and verse in translation."[45] The great poet Robert Frost has made my job easy by saying something worthwhile about poetry and Derrida taught me about the impossibility and necessity of translation. If poetry is the translation of emotions, then translation of poetry is the translation of emotions. In this section I shall present before you Dr. Ramesh Pokhriyal 'Nishank' as a translated poet in English. I am going to introduce to you two books, namely *The Seeds of Creation* and *The Darkness in Vanishing*. These two selections are translated by Dr. Chetana Pokhriyal. She is professor and Head of Department of English at MKP PG College, Dehradun. The *Darkness is Vanishing* is a translation of *Andhera ja Raha Hai* and *The Seeds of Creation* is a translation of *Srijan ke Beej*.

Poetry is what gets lost in translation. What a unique way to define poetry! I start this paragraph with these words because I received not one, but two volumes of poetry in translation. Dr. Chetana Pokhriyal translates Nishank, the poet and brings out *The Seeds of Creation* and *The Darkness is Vanishing*. I am flabbergasted!. If you don't know the meaning of the word 'flabbergasted', ask Shashi Tharoor. I have also translated a couple of novels and selections of poems into English and I know the difficulties of a translator. But as a reader, why should you go to these poems? Why do we read translated poetry? Will the poetry in translation allow me to appreciate the poet? Rajashekhar states that in the first *prahar* (quarter) of the day, the poet should study all forms of knowledge; the second *prahar* should be devoted to poetic composition; the third to 'stimulating talk' and 'questions, answers, and counter-questions'. A poet is supposed to have the following—a strong constitution (*sasthya*), a good memory (*smritidardhya*) and the ability to not be disappointed soon (*anirveda*). He doesn't say what he should do in his fourth *prahar*. I would like to say that he should translate during the time left.

The French poet, Francis Ponge says, "All objects yearn to express themselves, and they mutely wait the coming of the word so that they may reveal the hidden depths of their being."[46] The target reader of these books is naturally one who doesn't know Hindi and may also be unfamiliar with the source poet. It is the job of the translator to first introduce the poet to the reader and then his poetry. She does it well in the translator's Preface. In fact, when she 'naturally picked up a collection of small poems *Andhera ja Raha Hai* by Shri Ramesh Pokhriyal 'Nishank' for translation into English, she wondered and exclaimed, 'What is it all about?' She understood everything after close reading and then translated the book, poem by poem. As always, the preface was written after the translation was completed and the reader finds it to better understand the poet.

> "As a poet, Nishank surveys the possibilities, compares them to the actualities, facts, theories, the alternatives and the ideal, and weighs them together. Hence, they are both insightful and foresighted to make a sense of worth of life. Amazing is the fact, that these poems are not complex but simple and pliable and the doctrines

> and practices endorsed in them are not something new and recent but in tandem with the established norms."[47]

I am not going to provide a bulk of the translated ones from 138 poems. It is neither possible nor desirable. Let me give you just one as follows:

> Yet
> Your deals.
> Even your deals
> Are somewhat strange
> This is a destiny only to some.
> With a shower of your slightest smile
> You win over us
> For life.[48]

The reader will appreciate when Dr. Chetana translated Dr. Nishank's poetic sensibility by her erudite wisdom and used 'shower of your slightest smile'. The job of the translator is not only of a postman but also of a creative reader and lyricist. In a similar fashion, in *The Seeds of Creation*, the translator very adroitly puts forward Dr. Nishank's 'astutely conscripted sentiments of a nation and intrinsic human values.' She reminds the readers of the view of Benedict Anderson, who identifies national utopian and existential spaces. Let me also add Anderson's *Imagined Communities* for better clarification. A nation is a community because:

> "Regardless of the actual inequality and exploitation that may prevail in each, the nation is always conceived as a deep, horizontal comradeship. Ultimately it is this fraternity that makes it possible, over the past two centuries, for so many millions of people, not so much to kill, as willingly to die for such limited imaginings."[49]

This is the translator's point of view that 'the poet imagines India and its art as culture and national identities. Hence, India imagined through the poems in *The Seeds of Creation* is holy, virtuous, romantic and intrinsically national, which is ancient. The poet fights the visible threats to the imagined nationalism through iridescent plethora of human values in the Indian culture through all his poems in this collection.'[50] Nearly 100 poems translated are said to be "replete with charming, inspirational and sublime thinking."[51]

I shall prefer to offer the following translated piece which is a poem number one in the list and is titled *Let Me be So*.

Like the petals of the lotus
Even while submerged
Live detached from water
Neither for itself
Store water, but from them
Stream flow,
Even amidst the humdrum of politics
Let me be so.
Expended daily with mind and soul
To exist as the creation germ.[52]

Needless to say, the reader shouldn't go and needn't go to these poems in translation for poetic fervour and prosodic features. One should let one's eyes advance towards the printed pages to grapple the meaning of life and the mind of the poet, who originally creates them. Dr. Nishank's translator has to acknowledge, as all translators must, that a translator is a traitor (*traduttore traditore*) and he/she may have to distort the literal meaning to convey emotional and aesthetic feelings. As George Steiner observed in After Babel: "The translator invades, extracts, and brings home."[53]

□

5

Nation, Narration and Nishank

Nations, like narratives, lose their origins in the myths of time and only fully realise their horizons in the mind's eye.
—*Homi K. Bhabha*

Nation stands for the community of people whose singular identity comes along with a commonly shared territory and government. In literature, especially in fiction, the nation is an attractive and inevitable ingredient to discuss. In a seminal work on *Nation and Nationhood: Imagined Communities: Reflections on the Origin and Spread of Nationalism*, Benedict Anderson views that the novel is perhaps the most suitable apparatus to embody national imagination as it has the technical resources to conjure up an "imagined community that is the nation". Homi Bhabha opines that Benedict Anderson's idea of "imagined communities significantly paved the way for the concept of Nation and Narration. Once Indians became 'We, the people' with our constitution and republic and our national identity was reaffirmed, our intelligentsia got the hint, loud and clear. Ngugi wa Thiong'o in his book *Decolonising the Mind* endorses Anderson's view. He goes a step further and says that "language carries culture, and culture carries, particularly through orature and literature, the entire body of values by which we come to perceive ourselves and our place in the world."[1] In other words, both nation and language help each other to present a national narration.

The history of the birth of Indian novel or novel in India begins in 1860-1870 and its subsequent progress indicates that the novelists also paved the way for unifying India into an emotional entity. *Anand Math* (The Abbey of Bliss) is a novel written in 1882 by Bankim Chandra Chateerjee. It gave us the clarion call for freedom and *vande mataram* (hail to the mother) became a salutation for the masses. Such novels have been providing us the foreground and background in narrating the nation. I do not mean that before this India, that is Bharat, was not considered as a united whole. It was there, but its narration was not so much underlined in the vernacular languages. Gandhiji wrote a small book *Hindi Swaraj* in 1909 in the form of a dialogue between a 'reader' and an 'editor' in which Gandhiji himself is posed as the editor. In the following passage, he is trying to put forward his idea of a nation. Let us begin this chapter with the following dialogue from the book:

> *Reader:* But I am impatient to hear your answer to my question. Has the introduction of Mahomedanism not unmade the nation?
>
> *Editor:* India cannot cease to be one nation because people belonging to different religions live in it. The introduction of foreigners does not necessarily destroy the nation: they merge into it. A country is one nation only when such a condition obtains in it. That country must have a faculty for assimilation. India has ever been such a country.[2]

This is made amply clear by Gandhi that as far as the idea of India is concerned, it has been there since the haze of antiquity. There are only a few scholars who claim that India has never been a nation. The other question is related with our realisation of it. Ananda Kentish Coomaraswamy (1877-1947), the great historian and art critic, says that each race has its own *svabhav* or nature and accordingly people and poets express themselves to create an atmosphere of togetherness among her people.

> *"Each race contributes something essential to the world's civilisation in the course of its own self-expression. The essential contribution of India is simply her Indianness; her great humiliation would be to substitute or to have substituted for his own character (svabhava) a cosmopolitan veneer, for then indeed she must come before the world empty-handed."*[3]

In the light of these remarks, India has ever been a nation and the national aspirations have been expressed by social reformers, politicians and men of letters. What I have written above is the foundation on which Nishank's entire work can be evaluated and appreciated. He writes to provide opportunities to the readers and intellectuals for a fruitful discussion with a view to underlining the inherent nationalistic fervour in his texts. When Dr. Ramesh Pokhriyal 'Nishank' defines and discusses his views about literature as such, he is in fact placing his ideas about the nation and her narration to indicate this.

> साहित्य मनुष्य को खंडित करनेवाली दृष्टियों से सदा विलग और सर्वोच्च होता है। पराधीनता के दिनों में भी राष्ट्र-भक्ति से ओत-प्रोत गीतों की गुनगुनाहट ने सारे राष्ट्र को जाग्रत् किया था और एक से बढ़कर एक लोगों में उत्सर्ग की भावना को पैदा किया था। आज पुनः विस्मृत होते उस अतीत को हम स्मरण करें और दुनिया को बतला दें कि हमारी मातृभूमि अपनी गहरी निद्रा त्याग चुकी है। अब उसे कोई रोक नहीं सकता, कोई बाह्य शक्ति उसे दबा नहीं सकती, स्वार्थी तत्त्व उसे भ्रमित नहीं कर सकते, न उसे जाति-पंथ के रूप में बाँटा जा सकता है और न उसे क्षेत्रवाद, भाषावाद, धर्म, व अलगाववाद के जहर को फैलाकर विभाजित किया जा सकता है।[4]
>
> (Literature is always segregated and supreme from the views that break men from men. Even during the days when India was not free, the lilting songs filled us with patriotic feelings and awakened the whole nation and instilled in us a feeling of emancipation. Today, let us remember those foregone-days that are slowly being

forgotten and tell everyone that our motherland has already left her deep slumber. Now no one can stop her, suppress her, no selfish elements can confuse her, neither can she be divided into caste, creed, religion, community, nor can she be divided by spreading the poison of regionalism, linguistic narrow-mindedness, and religious fundamentalism.)

Before I delve deeper into his work, let me give you a broad perspective of India's unity within her diversity. If the idea of composite India began with 1857, the idea of diverse India starts taking shape in 1947. 'Unity in diversity' became the *mantra* to invoke Bharat Mata. Leslie Fiedler's comment on the North American novel, *The Country and the Novel were Born Together* can be applied to the Hindi novel as fictional texts written after 1860 as novels got a literary status in Hindi too. Form the early novels in India, till date, there has been an assumption that a novel is a borrowed genre and Indians have been basically story-tellers of repute with *Panchtantra* and other stories at their composite credit. From the early days of Premchand, the novelists tried to depict the lives of the poor and the wretched of the earth and didn't bother much about fantastic, marvellous or wonderful. Ramesh Pokhriyal 'Nishank', as a novelist and story teller, follows the conventions set by Premchand, Goura Pant Shivani and Himanshu Joshi, just to name a few in his field.

Devotion and Dedication for the Motherland

During his formative years when Dr. Nishank started writing poetry and his poetic fervour was being presented in the form of books, a collection of his poems appeared with a foreword by Nand Kishore Dondhiyal 'Arun'. The very first sentence of the foreword of this selection ran as follows:

> जननी और जन्मभूमि स्वर्ग से भी बढ़ कर हैं।
> (Mother and motherland, both have been very proudly placed above the heaven is an oft-quoted dictum.)

The proficient scholar was able to underline the element of patriotic and nationalistic fervour in Dr. Nishank's poetry. This is also to be noted that the foreword was written on 19-5-1983. Ramesh Pokhriyal 'Nishank' was a very young, budding and vibrant poet. It was felt by the critics and readers then that the poet was deeply infatuated with the idea of motherland and nationalism which constitute the core of his thinking and perspective. It seemed that the young poet wanted to devote his life for the sake of his motherland and mother tongue, and was getting himself prepared for greater roles in life through social work, politics and poetry. He was in the process of trying his hand in short story and fiction. The poet's *bhakti* for his motherland and his dedication to her are expressed in his short preface appropriately called, *Hirday Pukar* (Heart's Appeal)'. Let me quote from it:

> प्रत्येक भारतवासी में देशभक्ति कूट-कूटकर भर सके, भारत माँ का हर पूत राष्ट्रप्रेम से ओत-प्रोत हो, यह अत्यावश्यक है। राष्ट्रप्रेम के अभाव में भयंकर दूरगामी परिणाम होते हैं। जिनका मूल्य देश को सदियों तक चुकाना पड़ता है। किसी भी राष्ट्र को परिपुष्ट सशक्त व गौरवशाली बनाने के लिए त्याग, साहस, वीरता, नैतिकता, राष्ट्रीयता व समर्पण का भाव होना आवश्यक है। इन भावों की जागृति में राष्ट्रीय गीत एवं कविताओं की प्रमुख भूमिका रहती है। ये गीत व्यक्ति-व्यक्ति को राष्ट्रधारा में ही नहीं जोड़ते, बल्कि विपरीत परिस्थितियों में भी मार्ग निकलते हुए राष्ट्र-संकट में देशभक्त को बलिदान के लिए प्रेरित भी करते हैं। बस! हर भारतीय का नाता अपने पूर्वजों एवं देश की माटी से जोड़ता व देश के प्रति मर-मिट जानेवाले वीर सपूतों का पुनीत स्मरण करना ही मेरी इन कविताओं का भाव है।[5]
>
> (In every Indian the element of patriotism should be filled to the brim and every child of our motherland must be nationalistic; this is a must. Lack of such abiding love will have far-reaching consequences. The price we have to pay for this lapse has to be paid by us for centuries. To transform any nation into a strong

and proud country, it is necessary to have a sense of sacrifice, courage, valour, morality, nationality and dedication. Patriotic songs and poems play a major role in the awakening of these expressions. These songs and poems not only enrich every person and play a major role in the awakening of these expressions, but also can be instrumental in playing a significant role in developing a sense of engagement and devotion for the motherland. My poems are based on the themes of the connection with the soil of the country and with our noble ancestors and are meant to remember those who have laid down their lives for the sake of our motherland.)

Once Vajpayeeji, the poet-politician, in his own imitable style said this while releasing Dr. Nishank's book:

> सक्रिय राजनीति में रहते हुए भी जिस प्रखरता से डॉ. 'निशंक साहित्य के क्षेत्र में लगातार संघर्षरत एवं रचनारत हैं, वह आम आदमी के बस की बात नहीं है। मुझे डॉ. 'निशंक' की संघर्षशीलता और दृढ़ इच्छा-शक्ति पर पूर्ण विश्वास है कि वह अपने राजनीतिक जीवन की व्यस्तताओं के उपरांत भी अपनी लेखनी के माध्यम से आम जनमानस की भावनाओं को उभार कर समाज एवं देश के सामने ऐसे प्रश्न खड़े करते रहेंगे, जिनके उत्तर के लिए कभी-न-कभी जिम्मेदार व्यक्तियों को अपने कर्तव्यों का अहसास जरूर हो जाएगा।[6]
>
> (Despite being in active politics, the vigour with which Dr. Nishank is constantly struggling and creating new space for himself in the realm of literature can't be attained by an ordinary man. I have full faith in the struggle and strong will-power of Dr. Nishank that he will continue to raise such questions and issues before our society and country through his writings, so that the reactions and sentiments of the masses are made known to the people who are responsible to mitigate their woes also realise their duties towards them.)

Nationalism and Uttarakhand Region

Nobel-Prize-winning poet, Seamus Heaney, asks, "All around there is good writing but where is the great carrying voice of the definitive centre?"[7] In the globalised world, it is not advisable to talk about nation and region. But in literary criticism, we often take up and follow this point. In Hindi, *anchalik upanyas'* and *'anchalik kathakar'* are the two terms circulated around. In 1926, when Premchand was at his peak, Acharya Shiv Pujan Sahay wrote a novel, *Dehati Duniya* to depict the real world of the Indian typical village. The name of the village in *Dehati Dunia* is Ramsahar. Phanishwar Nath 'Renu' in his novel *Maila Anchal* brings out the dusty village of a region in the forefront. *Maila Aanchal* (The Soiled Border) is a 1954—Hindi novel written by Phanishwar Nath 'Renu'. After Premchand's *Godan, Maila Anchal* is regarded as the most significant Hindi novel in the Hindi literary tradition. It is one of the greatest examples of *'anchalik upanyas'* (regional novel) in Hindi. The depiction of reality of the imaginary or real region for which R.K. Narayan in English and Fakir Mohan Senapati in Oriya became so famous is still found in a few novelists, like Shivani and Himanshu Joshi. Dr. Nishank, as a novelist, can be studied along with and in the company of such great regional novelists, who have contributed enormously to the growth of Indian fiction. There is a recurrent theme in Nishank's novels and short stories that indicates that he very naturally and instinctively intertwines his region into his fiction. For Nishank, region is not a value but a device as he wants to reach globally through his locally-woven narrations.

Dr. Nishank depicts the life of the people living on the hilly terrain, making Uttarakhand a high priority. Even after so many years of Independence, our tribal population and others living there have to face mountainous difficulties. Governments come and go, but the people remain and their lives remain unaffected. Dr. Nishank feels the misery and pain with which the poor live and continue living in the fond hope of a better future. He has been a vocal mouthpiece for them and his fiction is based on the lives of the subaltern, who can't speak for themselves.

The portrayal of the immediate environment, the landscape and the flora and fauna of the hilly terrain of Uttarakhand contributes invariably to Dr. Nishank's poetic nationalism. He has been creating newer and more fascinating images and distinct idioms. Uttarakhand, with her greenery, environment, hills, pastures, and beautiful-but-difficult lives is a case in point. His is not the criticism of Indian life but a critical appreciation of it. Those who are enamoured of city life are not extolled by the poet but are asked to look back in repose.

The return of the native is a recurring theme of Dr. Nishank's novels. The desire of every youth to go out and serve in the Army is also a theme directly associated with the fervour of nationalism. In the novel *Pratigya* (2013), the theme is very clear and praiseworthy. Those who want to go out are told to take up some welfare work in their respective villages. It is true that life in the villages is tough and the city life is enticing and charming. There are other difficulties also.

Every work of fiction has characters, setting, plot, story, theme and narrative. Sometimes novelists create a *mouthpiece* in order to put forward their life or point of view. An 'author surrogate' or 'mouthpiece' is not uncommon in novels. A surrogate's life may be very similar to that of the author. Dr. Nishank has been picking up real-life characters and it is also a fact that he puts his views here and there along with the setting and plot. For instance, in the novel *Mere Sankalp*, the character of Narayan is shaped with his experience as a political person.

> राजनीतिक जीवन में दो बार मंत्री–पद पर रहने के बाद भी नारायण ने अपनी स्वच्छ छवि पर आँच न आने दी। भाई–भतीजावाद का आरोप न लगे, इसलिए उसने अपने परिवार के सदस्यों को राजनीति से दूर ही रखा। बच्चों को हमेशा अच्छी पढ़ाई व अपने पैरों पर खड़ा होने के लिए प्रेरित

> किया। इसी का परिणाम था कि दोनों बेटियाँ अपनी पढ़ाई पूरी करने के उपरांत स्वयं की योग्यता के बल पर उच्च पदों पर कार्यरत थीं।[8]
>
> (Even after being a minister twice in his political life, Narayan didn't allow his clean image to get tarnished. He shouldn't be accused of nepotism that was the reason that he kept the members of his family away from politics. He always motivated his offspring to study well and stand on their own. That was the reason that both the daughters, after completing their studies, were employed in high positions on the strength of their own abilities.).

There is a seamy side to political life and politics and it is not unknown to us. Even the word 'party-politics' is talked of in a derogatory sense. In the same novel, we have another character who is just the opposite of Narayan and who uses all the tricks at his disposal. Mavlesh's character is presented as follows:

> विधान सभा चुनावों में भी मवलेश का जादू युवाओं के सिर पर चढ़कर बोल रहा था, उसने पैसा और शराब पानी की तरह बहाकर लोकतंत्र की आत्मा को भी छिन्न-भिन्न कर दिया। आखिरकार शराब और रुपया नैतिक मूल्यों व ईमानदार प्रत्याशियों पर भारी पड़ गया और बड़ेथी का डकैत मवलेश प्रसाद चुनाव जीतकर विधायक बन गया। मवलेश की जीत को नैतिकता, सामाजिक शुचिता, उच्च मानवीय मूल्यों की पराजय के रूप में सामाजिक व राजनीतिक पर्यवेक्षक देख रहे थे।[9]
>
> (Even in the assembly elections, the magic of Mavlesh was prevalent on the youth's mind. He shattered the soul of democracy by spending money and giving away liquor like water. Eventually liquor and money power overshadowed moral values and honest candidates, and Mavlesh Prasad, the dacoit from Badaithi, won the election and became an MLA. Social and political observers were seeing Mavlesh's victory as a defeat of morality, social purity and all high human values.)

The Great Retelling of Uttarakhand Narrative

Uttarakhand is the 27th state carved out from the Himalayan districts of Uttar Pradesh in the northern part of India. It is very respectfully referred as the *Devabhumi* (land of the gods) as there are many temples, including Badrinath and Kedarnath and holy rivers like Gangotri and Yamunotri. The name Uttarakhand is derived from the Sanskrit words *uttar* meaning 'north', and *khaṇḍa* meaning 'land', altogether simply meaning 'northern land'. The residents of the state are generally called Uttarakhandi, or sometimes either Garhwali or Kumaoni by their region of origin. It is believed that Sage Vyasa scripted the great epic *Mahabharata* in the state. The official language of the state is Hindi and the classical language Sanskrit is also declared another official language. Uttarakhand's diverse ethnicities have created a rich literary tradition in languages, including Hindi, Garhwali, Kumaoni, Jaunsari and Tharu. As far as Hindi is concerned, there have been a number of notable authors and poets who have contributed immensely to the development of Hindi language and literature. Abodh Bandhu Bahuguna, Pitambar Dutt Badathwal, Ganga Prasad Vimal, Mohan Upreti, Shailesh Matiyani, Gaura Pant Shivani, Shekhar Joshi, Leeladhar Jagudi, Manglesh Dabral, Manohar Shyam Joshi, Ramesh Chander Shah, Ruskin Bond, Viren Dangwal and Jnanpith awardee and Sahitya Akademi fellow Sumitranandan Pant are some of the notable poets, writers, novelists and authors. Destiny brought India's Wordsworth, Ruskin Bond, here in the summer of 1963 and he has been living in Mussoorie since then. His depiction of the region has been lauded by his fans and readers spread around the world.

> "Cries of vendors and the smell of cattle and ripening dung, children playing hopscotch in alleyways or gambling with coins, scuffling in the gutter for a lost Anna... and the cows moving leisurely through the crowd, nosing around for paper and stale, discarded vegetables; the more daring cows helping themselves

> at open stalls. And above the uneven tempo of the noise came the blare of loudspeaker playing a popular piece of music."[10]

Ramesh Pokhriyal 'Nishank' is one among the resplendent galaxy of writers and poets hailing from the region, now called Uttarakhand. What he writes about his state in the preface of his book, *Vivekananda in the Himalayas*, is worth citing here:

"The ethereal splendour of the Himalayas makes Uttarakhand—the Devbhumi (the abode of the gods) and the *tapobhumi* (the abode of the saints) and a symbol of happiness, prosperity and peace along with development. The Ganges, as a vehicle of culture and prosperity, descends from this place as a source of life, salvation and knowledge. The state of Uttarakhand, with its unalloyed environment, nurtures the natural abundance of the Himalayas for the entire world."[11]

Dr. Nishank takes every opportunity to extol his surroundings and the examples and illustrations are spread in the length and breadth of his writing:

> "Uttarakhand, the land of soaring Himalayan peaks and steamy lowland jungles, is an integral part of this great nation. Revered as Dev Bhoomi—the land of gods, the state is home to many ancient temples and renowned ashrams. Encompassed by two major international borders (China and Nepal), a member of every family joins the Army to serve nation and contribute to peace and prosperity. Life at hill stations or peaceful country-sides may attract town and city dwellers. However, Life it very tough and challenging here. Despite facing challenges tougher and stronger as mountains, the people of Uttarakhand are always ready to serve and work towards the well-being of others. The simplicity and cooperative thinking of people here not only inspires well-being of Uttarakhand but also of the entire nation."[12]

Nationalism to Internationalism

As early as 1827, Johann Wolfgang von Goethe declared that the epoch of world literature was at hand and everyone must strive to hasten its approach. Some twenty years later, in *The Communist Manifesto*, Karl Marx would echo this sentiment when he too pronounced that the era of world literature had finally arrived. In India, we have been saying this from the very beginning. The world as a large joint family has been our motto. Here is a well-known *shloka* you would have already read or heard:

सर्वे भवन्तु सुखिन:सर्वे सन्तु निरामया: ।
सर्वे भद्राणि पश्यन्तु मा कश्चिद्दु:ख भाग्भवेत्॥

(May all be prosperous and happy! May all be free from illness!
May all see what is spiritually uplifting! May no one suffer!

Our scriptures are full of such *shlokas* and *vasudaiva kutumbkam* has been our clarion call. We still follow the path of world brotherhood. It is in our DNA. The following *shloka* is worth quoting in this regard:

त्यजेदेकं कुलस्यार्थे ग्रामस्यार्थे कुलं त्यजेत्।
ग्रामं जनपदस्यार्थे ह्यात्मार्थे पृथिवीं त्यजेत्॥

कुल के हितार्थ एक का त्याग करना, गाँव के हितार्थ कुल का, देश के हितार्थ गाँव का और आत्मकल्याण के लिए पृथ्वी का त्याग करना चाहिए। (One should abandon one individual for the sake of the family, abandon the family for the sake of the village and abandon the village for the sake of the nation and abandon the nation for the sake of the self.)

It is our innate desire and wish that we belong to a family. It is a *bhavna* that works and that *bhavna* takes it to *sadbhavna*: *Visv ka kalyan ho*! We take out nationalism and internationalism together. Dr. Nishank says:

> जब मातृभूमि है, तब माता है, दोनों ही अतुलनीय हैं, परंतु मूलाधार मातृभूमि है। ऐसी मातृभूमि के लिए वंदन, स्तवन तथा सर्वस्व समर्पण हमारा पुनीत कर्तव्य है। मातृभूमि के प्रति उत्कट प्रेम एक उदात्त भाव है और उत्कट भाव का अनुसरण करती बुद्धि होती है तो उसका सुंदर रूप और गौरव स्वत: बढ़ने लगता है। किसी समाज या देश की मातृभूमि की उन्नति के मूल में उस समाज या देश के लोगों की सोच का सब से अधिक योगदान रहता है।[13]
>
> (When there is the motherland, then there is the mother; both are incomparable, but the base is the motherland. Salutation, eulogy and total devotion to our motherland are our sacred duty. An ardent love towards the motherland is a sublime gesture and if the intellect follows the vibrant spirit, her beautiful form and pride automatically increase. The thinking of the people of that society or country contributes most to the progress of the motherland.)

The above statement echoes the well-known *shloka* from the *Ramayana* of Valmiki in which Lord Rama said to his brother Lakshaman, *"Janani janmabhumishcha swargadapi gariyasi.'* As a poet, story-teller and novelist and even a writer of self-help books, Dr. Nishank has been keeping in mind only one thing and that is his 'nation'. It will be too much to say but as *kavikul guru* Kalidas writes *Raghuvansham* to familiarise his readers with the great clan though in his opinion, he had little genius to do so, in the same vein Dr. Nishank goes about narrating the nation and national aspirations in his own modest ways. Through his narratives he emphasises the idea of international nationalism. He believes in an idea of nationalism in which loyalty to one's own nation does not entail the disavowal or denigration of the interests of other nations. The undercurrent of human values in his novels and short stories indicate Dr. Nishank's stance towards universal values, such as love and brotherhood. The following passage will serve well to substantiate my point:

"We, as humans, have always considered the Almighty, nature and the supreme as core creator of the universe. Whether atheist or theist, each one of us believes that there's one supreme creator of universe, who controls life. Consistent development and management of nature is only way one can learn to appreciate the beauty of all living and non-living creations existing in the universe. All type of art is a form of worship. Despite hectic schedule and deep involvement in the field of politics, social arena, education and journalism, I was never at rest to the infinite turmoil within me. Although with the grace of Almighty; it was easier for me to overcome all kinds of challenges faced in politics, various problems one faces in life from time to time and difficult situations. I couldn't forget some depressed and dejected individuals with whom I encountered from time to time. Some of these are characters of my stories. Their experiences, miseries and challenges have served as a base for my stories."[14]

□

6
Literary Realism in Indian Setting

'Do not read, as children do, to amuse you, or like the ambitious, for the purpose of instruction. No, read in order to live.'
— Gustave Flaubert

Literary realism attempts to represent familiar things as they are. Authors choose to depict everyday and banal activities and experiences, instead of using a romanticised or similarly stylised presentation. Realism in the arts is the attempt to represent the subject matter truthfully, without artificiality and avoiding artistic conventions, as well as implausible, exotic and supernatural elements. Stendhal (1783-1842), the French novelist, was not appreciated until the 20th century because of his realistic style; so he dedicated his writing to 'the happy few' who at least took the trouble to read him. He compares a novelist holding a lens and wandering around in search of stories to be retold.

> "Ah, Sir, a novel is a mirror strolling along the highway; at times it reflects the azure of the skies, and at others, the muddy potholes in the road. And the man who carries this mirror in his pack will be accused by you of being immoral! His mirror shows the mire and you blame the mirror! Rather blame that high road upon which the puddle lies, still more the inspector of roads who allows the water to gather and the puddle to form."[1]

I am using Stendhal's quote because one of our lesser understood novelists once used his name and words to start one of his novels. Pt. Upendranath '*Ashk*', in his novel *Shahar mein Ghoomta Aina* (1963, *In the city, a Wandering Mirror*) uses the above quoted paragraph. The idea of a novelist roaming around the streets was a wonderful one, picked up by many novelists in Hindi also. 'Literature is a mirror of life' has already become an oft-quoted dictum. Realism is equally dear to Dr. Ramesh Pokhriyal 'Nishank' too. That is why I invoke Stendhel and Upendra Nath '*Ashk*', both. Each period has a peculiar pervasive *yug-dharma* (the ideal distillation of people's taste). Ugra specialises in a kind of sensational fiction too but Nishank is free from that. That is why their comparison as novelists can't be stretched too far.

In order to get some sense of Dr. Nishank's novels, I started reading the blurb of each novel I collected. Blurbs can be of immense help for the prospective buyer and reader. The blurbs I received were consistently author-centred and the effect of such praise has been opposite, as if the text produced by the author is subordinate to him and it is under his command to do what he has done for the story. As said by a critic: 'The life of the novel is blotted out by the focus on the 'life' of the author.'

When we study a novel or any text, we come across a dictum—literature is the mirror of life. Dr. Ramesh Pokhriyal 'Nishank' is such a novelist who has taken the task of a man with a mirror, wandering in his little heaven, called Uttarakhand. He is a novelist who doesn't invent characters from the figment of his imagination. He finds them in the course of his own struggle and challenges in life. They are his fellow travellers with their tales of weal and woe in their lives. Dr. Nishank, as a novelist, tries his level best that the readers' attention is directed neither on the protagonist's previous birth nor the next one. He wants to make his and her birth successful and happy.

Putting Readers at Ease

Novel is the most inclusive of the genres of prose in literature. It includes autobiography, biography, memoirs, sketches, reportaz, etc. and if the novelist is a poet also, then the intensity of feelings in his writing increases automatically. This is true of Dr. Nishank's fiction as well. Confident Nishank has the knack of putting his readers at ease as he writes the stories of his readers and his novels revolve around the life of those who try to make both ends meet just to lead a dignified life. There is no place for complacency in his fiction; his nationalism and love for his culture and values permit him only to create characters who are there to protect and guide others.

When I was in search of a suitable title for this chapter, I was very confused. Nishank is a prolific writer. He has been writing short stories, novels, travelogues, self-help books, biographies, poems, and is busy churning out books with an amazing speed. It is very difficult to give all of it a composite name or a title. I was also tempted to use a noun as an adjective to form and coin a new word, a new collocation: Raconteur Nishank. I have taken this word from Hans Raj 'Rahbar', a novelist and short-story writer who wrote a beautiful book in 1957 on Premchand. In the book, *Premchand: His life and Wrk*, he writes as follows: "Though not the focus of attraction, Premchand was the finest friend and raconteur a man could find. He had a knack of putting others at ease..." Therefore, Dr. Nishank can be given this sobriquet as 'Rahbar' gave to Premchand.

Once Dr. Nishank attended a conference at *Dakshin Bharat Hindi Prachar Sabha*, Hyderabad and those who attended it told me about his mild and courteous manners and the ability to put the others at ease is still being remembered by all of them. Similarly, Dr. Chandan Kumar, who teaches Hindi at Delhi University, said to Kritika Sharma, in an interview which appeared in *The Print* (7 June, 2019), "...But he is definitely someone who connects with people through his writing. The idea of India and patriotism reflects very well through his books. Books like *Bheed Sakshi Hai* and *Pahad se Uncha*, both novels have connection with the common man, especially *Pahad se Uncha* which is all about self-confidence." One who connects with people thorough his narrative is a raconteur. Dr. Nishank is one such novelist and story-teller.

Once in Virginia Woolf's drawing room, Mulk Raj Anand was mocked by a young critic for trying to write a novel about a Dalit. The novel was *Untouchable* (1935). It was the time when Premchand was writing his magnum opus *Godan* (1936) and Raja Rao was finalising his novel *Kanthapura* (1938). The preface of the novel *Untouchable* was written by E.M. Forster where he said, "None of us is pure—we shouldn't be alive if we were. But to the straightforward, all things can become pure." E.M. Forster was a genius. Munshi Premchand got a chance to read his book, *Aspects of the Novel* (1927) and he tried to absorb some of the points discussed by this genius. Nishank is one such novelist who is pure and simple when he writes about the villagers who live far away from the maddening crowd.

I am neither a genius nor a scholar, but I love mentioning those who are geniuses. I am a careful reader only. I cannot find out anything without reading. The novelist tells a story. I am like Scheherazade's husband as I want to know what happens next. I read a novel as Azar Nafisi in her book *Reading Lolita in Tehran* suggests—"This is how you read a novel. It is the sensual experience of another world. You inhale the experience." I inhale the experience and then the experience directs me to write these lines. I meander hither and thither in search of meaning in this disorganised word to earn your goodwill. As 'there is no literature without a suspended relation to meaning and reference', Jacques Derrida has already indicated. As a reader of literature—Nishank's literature—my search for meaning in his realistic portrayal of life is going to be based on the criteria adopted and recommended by E.M. Forster. That is why this lengthy background.

New Myth-maker Nishank

The great Wessex novelist, Thomas Hardy used to be very pessimistic in his novels and always left a tragic impression on his readers, but Dr. Nishank, as a novelist and story-teller, is perhaps following the dictum of 'poetic justice' with some exceptions. 'If you do well, you will receive well' is his motto.

"The past is a foreign country; they do differently things there." The immortal first line to L.P. Hartley's *The Go-Between*, wistfully condenses the problems inherent to memory and history. David Lowenthal in his book, *The Past is a Foreign Country* (1985) says that the past and future are grossly inaccessible. Though beyond physical reach, they are integral to our imagination. Reminiscences and expectations suffuse every present movement. Past and future attract—and repel—in quite different ways. Most images of time ahead are hazy and uncertain. We cannot even know the consequences of our own acts, let alone foretell the larger future. Dr. Ramesh Pokhriyal 'Nishank' is a politician-cum-writer. But once upon a time, during his days of struggle when the future was not as clear and transparent as it is now, he used to write with both the hands. His choice of subject and characters is based on life's real people. He himself says in '*Nivedan*' of his novel, *Pratigya* as follows:

> मैंने पौराणिक मिथकों को तोड़कर आम जन-जीवन को नायकत्व प्रदान किया है।[2]
>
> (I have given the place of pride and heroship to the routine life, breaking the bond of traditional myths around us.)

From the very beginning, the novelists in India have preferred 'real' than 'fantastic'. Though Dr. Nishank is well-aware of our traditions and culture, yet his novels and stories are not based on mythological characters. He is not in the field to tell us the age-old Puranic tales of adventure and feats of our past lives. The inventive power of an Amish Tripathi to portray events and characters that happened thousands of years ago is missing here. For him, the human beings that come into his contact directly and indirectly are the subjects and characters of his fiction.

Myths are the stories a culture tells to explain big things, like the origins of the universe, why the sky is blue and so on. A myth involves gods or supernatural elements. The characters are mainly gods and goddesses and those who have qualities fit to be like them. But Dr. Nishank's protagonists are not like Lord Rama and antagonists don't follow the evil of a Ravana. We shouldn't expect anything marvellous or wonderful in his not-so-bulky novels. His characters are the ordinary middle class and lower middle-class people trying to come up in life. He doesn't tell the story of a great politician who has made a mistake and suffered. Here are the young men and women like Veeru, Veer Singh of Madanpur, who want to change the course of their lives. Dr. Mohan, in the novel *Pahad se Uncha* is the protagonist who is an epitome of the life in Uttarakhand. I could scarcely find a character in his novels that is an out and out evil. I am tempted to say that wherever he meanders in his novels and short stories, he always returns to the Himalayas and River Bhagirathi.

Literary Realist Nishank

Fiction is 'the nearest thing to life' as George Eliot once said. "Art is the nearest thing to life. It is a mode of amplifying experience and extending our contact with our fellow-men beyond the bounds of our personal lot." Fiction isn't the same as life, but it is very close to it. Poets, dramatists and novelists and others, all live in the realm of fancy. They sing the songs of 'what is not'. For them, past and future are more important than the immediate present. The literary theorist and writer Susan Sontag draws on Albert Einstein when she argues that 'time exists in order that everything doesn't happen all at once' and 'space exists so that it doesn't all happen to you', and by this standard 'the novel is an ideal vehicle of time and space'.[3] One of Shakespeare's characters says, 'Oh, call back yesterday... Bid time return.'[4] *The Paradox of Time*, as the late poet Henry Austin Dobson summarises, is not that time passes quickly, but rather 'Alas, Time stays, we go.' Nishank, as a novelist and story-teller, is aware of this and lives in the present. One of the characters in his novel says:

> हम इनसान अपना वर्तमान कभी नहीं जीते। छोटे रहते हैं तो बड़ों को देखकर उनके जैसा बनने की कल्पना करते हैं। बड़े होते हैं तो आगे बढ़ने की कल्पना करते हैं। हम हमेशा आगे ही देखते हैं। जो सामने है, उसे कभी नहीं जीते और जब जीवन के अंतिम पड़ाव में होते हैं, तो मुड़कर पीछे देखते हैं। अपने बचपन और जवानी को याद करते हैं। यानि आगे और पीछे देखने में ही हमारा वर्तमान समाप्त हो जाता है।[5]
> (We, the humans, never live in the present. When young, we look towards the old and dream to be like them. The elders always dream to march forward. What is before them, they never live the moment. And when they grow old in the last leg of their lives, they turn back and recollect their days spent during childhood and youth. In other words, our present is spent only to look back and forth.)

The above-quoted lines indicate that the novelist is trying to present the philosophy of his life on which his themes of novels rest. It is also to be noted that Dr. Nishank is in the vocation of creative writing with a solid purpose and consolidated aim. He has the talent and genius to employ for his portrayal of the lives around him. I am not vain and superficial in using these adjectives. I am serious and concerned. E.M. Forster, in his path-breaking book, Aspects *of the Novel* (1927) writes that literature is written by geniuses and novelists are geniuses. Genius doesn't mean that the man has excessive talent. The word 'genius' is derived from the Latin word *gignere* (to beget) and a genius is a person who gives something which is original.

He creates what others couldn't create before. In this sense, Dr. Nishank is a talented man because of his genius. In other words, you can say that he is a writer of worth because of his talent and original genius. He is a genius because he doesn't waste his talent on insignificant pursuits. For Henry Fielding, one of the early English novelists, the genius required by the novelist involved what he called 'invention' and 'judgement'. The novelist must employ 'judgement' to discover the true essence of life.

Dr. Nishank focuses on the social reality of the Uttarakhand people. He is a novelist with a purpose. Realism for him is *mise en scene* (the setting or surroundings of an event). He writes from his personal experience and the experiences he gains by interacting with real people. For him, the novel is the medium of expression of humanism with a view to helping the disadvantaged group of our society. He writes about all classes of society but the lower- and middle-class life is largely in focus. He follows the simple Indian tradition of storytelling with no frills attached. His themes and events described in his novels are based on social realism. Therefore, his novels are the novels of social realism based on a particular region. A close study of the novels of Dr. Ramesh Pokhriyal 'Nishank' reveals that the social concerns that are portrayed in his novels are experienced by him in his rocky childhood and impressionable youth. He is a novelist with a clear-cut mission. He has a keen desire to instruct, to preach, to teach and to guide. By his novels, he teaches the principles of humanity and human values.

Dr. Nishank insists upon the dignity of every man. For him, this is the ultimate value. Anyone who surveys his novels or reads any of these novels just for time-pass cannot miss the novelist's deliberate attempts to expose and discuss the continual hard life and distress of his people. The people who have been struggling to make both ends meet but lead a life of repose and dignity are the different characters of his novels. He is a novelist for the people, by the people and of the people.

The novel *Pahad se Uncha* (Higher than the Mountain) tries to retouch a major and recurrent theme of his stories and novels. Back to his roots or back to village life is being portrayed as a panacea for so-many ills prevalent in the society. The author stands out as an authoritative expert on native legends and traditions. A research scholar can easily pick up all the references of festivals, folk-songs, dances, food, superstitious beliefs, daily routine, social cohesion, economic deprivation, women empowerment and otherwise, etc. and present these to get a diploma or degree. The anthropological study of these novels may also bring out bewildering results. Eco-critical and eco-feminist study of the novels will indicate the novelist's concerns for environment degradation and the measures we can take to stop the menace of felling the trees.

The novel, *Apna Paraya* (Mine and Yours) too becomes a mirror of life on the hillside. It is the story of Laxmi and Suresh and Rahul, Anita and Rashmi. Laxmi is the central character and the daily routine of the characters is presented in such an ordinary way that the effect becomes extraordinary. Here is a novelist who writes about the day-to-day life in such a modest way that the life of the ordinary people with their own small happiness and sorrows and pains and pleasures lead the reader to think deeply about the everlasting question of 'it's mine and it's yours'. We have been listening since childhood the dictum, '*idam namam*' which simply means 'it's not mine'. The entire world is in the vortex of *maya* and we are shrouded in mystery. It's our vocation to unravel it. The novel treats this philosophical thought in such a way that we are not only entertained but also educated.

Dr. Nishank has not taken up an avant-garde form for his novels. He has neither followed the stream of consciousness technique nor magic realism. He has his own self-imposed limit and no novel he has written till now exceeds 200 pages. They are all written on the themes related to values and *sanskar* so dear to Indians. He writes as if he has a life -mission to present his characters in the form of stories that teach and preach at the same time. On the whole, the true value of Dr. Nishank's stories lie not in their realism with a setting of an area known as Uttarakhand but on the characters that are reader-like and out of the dusty terrains of mundane life in which words of wisdom flow uninterrupted. His art is traditional and conservative in strategy but is steeped in humane realism. His characters may be fictional but the special feelings and emotion they create in the mind and heart of the readers is because they have been taken from the real world.

The novelist is himself a human being. He has an affinity with the characters he portrays. He has seen them somewhere. Growing frustration sometimes make his characters rebel against the social customs and traditions. There are so many problems in the villages. Young boys, once educated, go to cities to earn their livelihood. For instance, in *Pratigya*, Veeru and Kuldeep, the protagonist and the antagonist, respectively belong to different worlds. They are poles apart. Kuldeep is evil incarnate but Veeru is killed. In another novel, *Pahad se Uncha* the character of Dr. Mohan reminds us of our very own A.P.J. Abdul Kalam. Similarly in *Pallavi* the novelist creates an ideal character as Dhruv and insolent characters as Bindu and the advocate. Dhruv is a typical man of his salt.

The main facets in human life are five: birth, food, sleep, love and death. They play a part in our real life and they play a part in the novel also. It is the skill of the novelist that he presents these events in the life of his characters. In Hindi, we look at a novel according to its *kathavastu* (story), *paatr* (character), *uddeshya* (purpose), *kathopakathan* (dialogue), *deshkaal* (place and time), *bhasha-shaili* (language and style), but in English, the trend is different.

Art of Characterisation

The backbone of a novel has to be a story. And a story is a story. Can Nishank tell a story? I didn't get a chance to count the stories written by Dr. Nishank, but what I got to read is enough to say something worthwhile. Nishank, as a story-teller, specialises in narrating stories of our society's miseries, pains, hypocrisy, exploitation, etc. The compassionate side of life percolates in his writing. His is no magic realism, adventure or steamy love and romance. The hard facts of life without a tinge of negativity are spread with a purpose. You can call it life-values, if you like, but it is not restricted to values. There are many shades without a shade of grey. The life sparkles here and even in the depiction of flood and human tragedies, the writer in Dr. Nishank is careful to present his characters in such a way that the happiness becomes a recurrent episode amidst occasional traces of pain and tragic moments.

Do you know who Manoj Santoshi is? Do you know Happu Singh? Happu Singh is a character imagined by the writer Manoj Santoshi. Happu Singh is a minor character in a TV sit-com who later became the main character of another sit-com. This is about television shows. Harry Potter is known to so many but how many know the name of his creator, J.K. Rowling? Character is the life-blood of literature. For Harold Bloom, a literary character is always an invention, and inventions generally are indebted to prior inventions. We remember them as much as the novelist who creates them. We identify with them and have sympathy and antipathy for them accordingly. The plot of a story or a novel is largely for the sake of the characters who speak their mind as the author desires. We remember a novel because we remember the characters. We, as readers, 'identify' with characters in novels and stories. We enjoy a novel when we identify with the characters in it. We don't like a character with whom we fail to identify. In other words, we are always in search of our self and once we find such a man or woman who resembles us, we declare the novel successful. For instance, when we read the novel *Pallavi*, we start identifying with the protagonist Dhruv and those who are women, they wish to be like the main female character Pallavi. This appreciation and acknowledgement and identification go a little far when even the critics start associating a character with the novelist who created it.

Dr. Nishank as a novelist has a definite purpose and he tells his story, keeping in mind the values he wishes to inculcate in his readers. But he is not a social reformer. He is neither a philosopher nor a socialist. He is a story-teller who creates characters taken from real life and surroundings. His characters don't belong to the entire humanity or in other words, we can say that his characters are not pan-Indian. They belong to a particular region. The beauty of these characters lies in their universal appeal. Though he is still not frequently available in translation, yet any Indian who reads him will find those characters around him as they are the progeny of common humanity. As our life is an ebb and flow of sorrow and happiness, good and ill, Dr. Nishank's world presents a portal of life consisting of both. His characters are both flat and round. For instance, in the novel *Pallavi*, we have a character that is differently-abled. He is purposely named Shravan (who will not be aware of the boy Shravan Kumar?) and presented as an embodiment of positivity in life. The protagonist of the novel, Dhruv, who is an embodiment of goodness and mouthpiece of the novelist, does his best to let him progress in life. Pallavi's father Ramakant stands for elite and leisure-class person who is full of pride and vanity. He is blinded by his power and pelf and tries to guide his daughter to follow his instructions. Dr. Yogendra Nath Sharma 'Arun' is of the view that most of Dr. Nishank's characters are the embodiment of our life values and Prof. Rishabha Deo Sharma opines that this is because of the author's sublime persona. In criticism, the didactic purpose of a novel is earmarked by scholars, such as David Foster Wallace when he says that ultimately fiction is what it is to be a human being. Dr. Nishank as a novelist is not solving our burning problems but is able to suggest what the problems are and how the common people are coping with them. He gives us a ringside view of the hill-region beyond and including Haridwar. In the novel, *Chuut gaya Padav*, we find a village which is an exceptional one in the region with its vitality and richness but devoid of arrangement for education.

Anand Singh somehow gets a lady teacher named Saroj for the village school and this teacher transforms the entire village with her social work and education. Even the deaf and dumb daughter of Anand Singh finds in her a great help. Though this girl named Rani dies due to medical condition, yet her death gives Saroj firm determination to start an institution named Navjeevan. This novel reminds us of Thomas Hardy's Wessex novels in which human condition and destiny play a significant role. The author tries to admonish others through the clarion call given by Saroj. She asks everyone not to remain idle and solely depend on destiny and fate.

Dr. Nishank's fiction is a microcosm of calm but warm humanism spread in the God's county called Uttarakhand. Characters drawn from the rustic and hilly terrain may seem to you ordinary and commonplace but their portrayal with the brush of tenderness and concern make each of them sparkling with dialogues as natural and clear as the waters of the holy river, Bhagirathi.

> "आज फिर क्यों आया था वह यहाँ पर ?"
> "शादी करना चाहता है तुझसे।"
> "शादी करना चाहता है ? क्या समझा है उसने मुझे ? एक बार माँ-बाप मना करते हैं, तो दूसरी बार बेटा हाँ करने चला आता है। गुड्डे-गुड़िया का खेल है क्या ?"
> अपमान और क्षोभ से लक्ष्मी का चेहरा तमतमा आया।[6]
> ('Why did he come here today again?'
> 'Wants to marry you.'
> "Wants to get married? What has he understood me? Once the parents refuse, the second time the son comes to say 'yes'. Is marriage a child's play?"
> Laxmi's face turned red with insult and rage.)

The language used by the novelist is remarkable, not because of the use of local idiom but because it comes so naturally and effortlessly. It doesn't mean that here you can find the linguistic command and verbal combat of Manohar

Shyam Joshi or Himanshu Joshi. They were past-masters in the field. But look at the following lines and you will surely feel like borrowing words from John Keats, "Where are the songs of spring? Ah where are they? Think not of them, thou hath thy music too."

> भोर में झकझोर कर किसी 'पाहुन' के आने का पैगाम दे जाता 'कागा' आज न जाने क्यों मुँड़ेर पर मुँह फेरे बैठा था। नीचे पगलाई सी 'चंदा' अपना खूँटा उखाड़ डालने पर आमदा थी। दूर कहीं बिछड़े बछड़े की मर्मांतक पुकार कानों में पड़ते ही वह और बिलबिला उठी थी। पेट के भीतर कहीं गहराई से निकलती—'अम्माह''' अम्माह' की उसकी चीत्कार मानो कलेजा चीर रही थी।
>
> पास ही बूढ़ी हो चली 'बिंदा' पथराई सी खड़ी थी। सुबह से उसने आज तिनका तक मुँह में नहीं डाला। बस आँसू बहाए जा रही थी।[7]
>
> (Only God knows why the crow that used to scream messages at dawn on the arrival of the guest was sitting on the cornice keeping its beak turning the other way. Downright insane, Chanda was trying hard to uproot the peg with which she was tied. As soon as she heard the heart-wrenching bellow, she was more in pain than before. The yelling sound 'Ammah...Ammah...' coming out of the calf's very stomach was heard by the mother cow pierced her heart.
>
> Nearby old Binda stood stiff like a piece of stone. Not a morsel entered her mouth since morning. She was just shedding tears.)

Virginia Woolf wisely reminded us that novelists write not only in sentences but also in paragraphs and chapters. In a very famous story, *Kahani ka Plot*, Shivpujan Sahay tells us a secret of the story-tellers in the following lines:

> भाषा में गरीबी को ठीक-ठीक चित्रित करने की शक्ति नहीं होती, भले ही वह राजमहलों की ऐश्वर्य-लीला और विलास-वैभव के वर्णन करने में समर्थ हो।[8]

> (Language does not have the power to accurately portray poverty, even if it is able to describe the majesty and opulence of the palaces.)

Dr. Nishank is not depicting and portraying the power and pelf of the sophisticated elite of society. He has been living amidst the poor and the middle-class people who speak the language of the heart that is so earthy. The language used by Dr. Nishank is not ornate and full of 'purple passages' so fondly associated with D.H. Lawrence. The use of figurative language is not Dr. Nishank's forte. He eschews pedantry and verbosity. His language is simple and commonplace and there is hardly any attempt to use words that are lifted to show off. His language-flow is natural and simple, with a rich vocabulary of his region in which his characters live and interact. I fail to find the use of English words and expressions in his writing except where they come naturally, as in the following sentence: हैव यू गोन मैड ? तुम पागल हो गई हो ! (Have you gone mad?)

Women as Fulcrum

The position of women in our changing society has been a subject of our novels from the very beginning. In fact, the centrality of women in Dr. Nishank's novel is so common that we can't miss them juggling between traditional and modern values. In a society where the expectations from girls and women have been traditionally limited and obscure, Dr. Nishank's stories and novels put forward characters in the league of *Devrani Jethani ki Kahani* and not of *Pariksha Guru*. His are not the love stories in which the end comes with the notion of 'they lived happily ever after'. He depicts contemporary social realities of Indian life in general and the life of his region, in particular. A genuine literary critic can very easily find in his fiction an empowering text without a tinge of being so-called 'feminist'.

The credit of writing a notable book about feminism in Hindi fiction also goes to a man of letters. Rajendra Yadav writes:

> स्त्री हमारा अंश और विस्तार है। वह हमारी ऐसी जन्मभूमि है जिसे हमने अपना उपनिवेश बना लिया है। उन की मुक्ति स्वयं हमारी मुक्ति है। यानी गुलाम बनाए रखनेवाली मानसिक गुलामी से मुक्ति है।[9]
>
> (Woman is our part and extension. It is our birthplace in a way which we have colonised. In her liberation is our own salvation. That is, liberation from mental slavery which keeps it so.)

In the novels and stories by Dr. Nishank, the female characters are as powerful as the male. For instance, in the novel *Chuut Gaya Padav* the narrator has a realistic point of view when he says that our world has become self-centred and narrow and we fail to see beyond our family comprising a wife and children. The narrator is able to say through the protagonist Saroj what he wants. Even in his portrayal of Saroj's persona, he keeps his eyes fixed on her genius and not physical beauty.

> शिक्षा-संस्कारों का पावन संगम थी सरोज। जितनी प्रबुद्ध, उतनी ही विनीत। प्रखर भी और परिपक्व भी। एक सच्ची गुरु। बिल्कुल संत कबीर के कुम्हार-सी। जो घड़ा गढ़ने को अंदर तो हाथ का सहारा दे, और बाहर से चोट मारे। सुंदर घड़े को आकार देने की युगलबंदी बच्चों तक ही नहीं, उनके माँ-बाप पर भी लागू करती।[10]
>
> (Saroj was a sacred confluence of education and conventions. The more entitled, the more humble. Strong as well as mature. A true teacher. Absolutely like the potter of poet Kabir. One who supports from inside the pitcher with his expert hand. The *jugalbandi* (combination) of shaping the beautiful pitcher was confined not only to the children, but also to their parents.)

In another novel, *Pallavi,* we find that the character of Pallavi stands for an ideal woman of her surroundings. She stands for truth, sacrifice and bravery. In short, she is 'Mother India' incarnate. She is also a helping hand for differently-abled Shravan and gets inspired by the lofty character of Dhruv.

Nishank's feminism, if any, is embedded in his universal humanism that doesn't extol women for namesake. They are presented in such a way that the reader himself nods in approval and stands by their side. We mayl ask, "Can a man speak for a woman?" I argue that great authors are free from all this. Dr. Nishank speaks through his characters and the characters speak for women and their empowerment. In Dr. Nishank's novels, women are not as exalted as men, but ultimately they are able to make a mark by the dint of their perseverance and determination. That is why it should be conveniently said that Dr. Nishank is not a feminist in the strict sense of the term but he doesn't shy away from presenting his female characters as powerful as men.

Retelling Uttarakhand Tragedy

Pralay ke Beech (Amidst Catastrophe) is a new kind of book in which the style and genre, both are unique. The Kedarnath tragedy is the protagonist and the aim is not what Aristotle claimed centuries ago. Yes, the reader will get a different kind of purgation of the morbid element of pity and fear. It is not of the morbid element of pity and fear; it is of the horror of the tragedy, partly man-made and partly a divine curse.

> फिर न दिखाना ऐसे दिन केदार बाबा!
> चीख पुकार! हाहाकार! पीड़ा से तड़पते-बिलखते लोग, अपनों को ढूँढ़ते दौडते-भागते लोग! अफरा-तफरी जैसा माहौल। उफ! कोई भी व्यक्ति यह दृश्य देखता तो उसकी आत्मा सिहर उठती और वह स्वत: ही पागलपन की स्थिति में चला जाता। न जाने किस बात पर रुष्ट हो गए केदार बाबा![11]
>
> (Never let us witness such days Kedar Baba!
> Hue and cry! Commotion! People crying and wailing in pain, People running and searching for their dear ones! A chaotic atmosphere! Oops! If any person saw this terrible scene, his soul should have shivered and he

> would have automatically gone into a state of madness. Don't know why Kedar Baba became so angry with us!)

The rule of closure dictates its whole plot which means that some characters must die in a novel. The death scene is the last scene of *Godan* by Premchand is well known and a case in point. In fictional narratives, people come and go, die and perish. Dr. Nishank has not only seen personal tragedies like all human beings, but also has been a witness of certain deaths nobody would even think of. He lived amidst catastrophes. For instance, *Pralaya ke Beech* is not only a narrative, but also a true account of what happened. Here 'death' is not fiction; it is real and tragic. It's not the 'Kedarnath' film with a hidden story of a Muslim boy and a Hindu girl; it is what really happened.

> शरीर नजर आ रहे थे, जिनमें साँसे नहीं थीं। अब वे लाशें मात्र थीं। ये सब ही संबंधों और संवेदनाओं की परिधि से बाहर हो चुके थे। इनका क्या करें, कहाँ ले जाएँ इनको, कैसे इनका अंतिम संस्कार करें? इसके लिए कोई रास्ता नहीं है। अपनी ही आँखों के सामने अपना सबकुछ बरबाद होते देखते हुए भी लोग लाचार और विवश थे।[12]
>
> (The bodies were visible, they were not breathing. Now they were mere corpses. All these were outside the purview of relationships and feelings. What to do with them, where to take them, how to cremate them. There was no way for this. People were helpless and compelled to see everything wasting before their own eyes.)

There is another book *Aapda ke Vah Bhhayavah Din* (*Uttrakhand Aapda*, 2010) in which we get an eye-witness account of death and utter callousness of nature. Why will the reader read it now after a decade? It will be read because of its vivid descriptions of death and tragedy. It is the tragedy of others' lives that purges our morbid elements of pity and fear. Dr. Nishank's narrative power is the dominant strategy that gives this tragedy what is called 'repeat-value'. The readers are able to visualise the incident long after the people who are described start forgetting the ill-fated event. The telling of the story afterwards becomes important in its own way. Life goes on along with the stories of our past struggles and challenges. Dr. Nishank is able to take his readers as an escort. Without him, the events must have disappeared in the folklore and heresy. Therefore, his contribution as an eye-witness and author are commendable.

□

7

Long Story Short: Humanity Personified

We are all just stories in the end. Just make it a good one, eh?
—The doctor in Doctor Who

Writers and readers both see in a work of fiction 'each man's life a strange emblem of every man.' Fiction has been dominating literature in the twentieth century and beyond, leaving poetry far behind. In this century, the short story seems to win the race or is still ahead of other genres of literature. Nabokov, in his *Lectures on Literature*, extols the virtue of fiction and does not like to compartmentalise them into novel and short story. He says, "Fiction is fiction. To call a story is an insult to both act and truth." A writer can be considered as a story-teller, as a teacher and as an enchanter. A good writer combines these three together—story-teller, teacher and enchanter. Those who have the third one in the highest ratio are greatest of the great. Let us see how far Dr. Nishank goes as a story-teller. Dr. Nishank has published not less than 15 collections of his stories. Those who read him find in his stories humane and human sensibilities. The avid readers say that his fiction is not merely fiction but factual representation in the garb of stories. Let us read what Dr. Nishank says about his art and craft as a story-teller:

"We, as humans, have always considered the Almighty, nature and the supreme as core creator of the universe.

Whether atheist or theist, each one of us believes that there's one supreme creator of universe, who controls life. Consistent development and management of nature is the only way one can learn to appreciate the beauty of all living and non-living creations existing in the universe. All types of art are a form of worship. Despite hectic schedule and deep involvement in the field of politics, social arena, education and journalism, I was never at rest due to the infinite turmoil within me. Although, with the grace of Almighty, it was easier for me to overcome all kinds of challenges faced in politics, various problems one face in life from time to time, and difficult situations, yet I couldn't forget some depressed and dejected individuals with whom I came into contact, from time to time. Some of these are characters of my stories. Their experiences, miseries and challenges have served as a base for my stories."[1]

Wandering Mirror

I am tempted to compare Dr. Ramesh Pokhriyal 'Nishank' with another Hindi novelist and story-teller, Pt. Upendranath Sharma '*Ashk*' (1910-1996). Daisy Rockwell and Diana Dimitrova had written about '*Ashk*' in English. Let me quote a translated piece originally written by '*Ashk*' and translated by Rockwell:

> "But the question is, in this age of struggle, for whom does the story-teller write? Does he write for the wealthy and aristocratic writers or critics of today, who now take the place of Kalidas's maharajas, or does he write for the thousands of people engaged in struggles just like him? Kalidas and his contemporaries lived under the patronage of rajas and maharajas; they created literature solely for the enjoyment of their masters, and what would be the use of sickness, sorrow, poverty, the tiny, aggravating details of life that leave a bitter taste in one's mouth—those utterly

ordinary, negligible events—to a raja? Some of our critics even see themselves as the rajas and hold similar expectations of the writer. But if the writer doesn't write for them, if he writes for thousands of other mud-smeared souls, like himself, then clearly he won't show them the beauty of the lotus but all the other items in the lotus tank: the spreading roots, the mud, the slime, the weeds and all the other matter the writer wishes to clean from the tank—all of it—all such items are responsible for the spread of countless germs of illness and filth, whether five lotuses happen to bloom there or ten."[2]

The above views expressed by '*Ashk*' in the preface to his novel, *Girti Deevaren* (Falling Walls) are being followed in the following lines written by Dr. Nishank in the preface of his collected stories. What Nishank thinks about the art of fiction and story-telling can also be gauged from the following lines:

> कहानियाँ हमारे जीवन संसार के इंद्रधनुषी रंगों का सार-संकलन भर ही नहीं होतीं, ये देखे, महसूस किए और भोगे ताप-संताप को जीवंत दस्तावेज भी देती हैं। हमारा हौसला बढ़ाती है और गाहे-बगाहे रास्ता भी दिखाती हैं। कभी मन कुरेद कर सही-गलत की हामी भरवाती हैं, तो कभी हमें हमारी जिम्मेदारी व दायित्वों का बोध भी कराती हैं।[3]
> (The stories are not only a compendium of rainbow colours of the substance of our life-experiences. It also gives a lively document of our perception, feelings and experience. It gives us encouragement and also shows us the way from time to time. Sometimes, it gets us inspired to do good and well, sometimes make us realise our responsibilities and duties to do good.)

In another preface of his selected stories, he is more specific than before and talks about decaying values and traditions as the subjects of his stories:

> इस कहानी-संग्रह में क्षरित होते हुए मूल्यों-परंपराओं, ऊष्माहीन रिश्तों, दम-तोड़ती हुई संवेदनाओं, संघर्षों, विडंबनाओं और विद्रूपताओं को मर्मांतक ढंग से चित्रित किया गया है।[4]
>
> (In this selection of stories, one can find a careful depiction of depleting human values and traditions, valueless relations, dying sensibilities, all-pervading conflicts, irony and rebellion.)

The very first story of this collection, is '*Jag ki Reet* (The Ways of the World) and it tells us how the institution of joint families is being shattered by the new generation. Dr. Nishank's stories are also like a mirror wandering around the cities, towns and villages to capture vivid images of life which is no longer as it should have been. He will very dexterously weave a story around breaking news and the reader will follow his lines as if he has already seen all that and it is only a journalistic account of it. During his youth and struggle days, Dr. Nishank was a journalist also and he had been observing incidents happening around. That knack of picking up stories has helped him in his narration. It is up to the critic to pinpoint in his stories the various facets of life and different discourses but an average reader goes to him to get a slice of life in which he himself is a character.

The readers of this book will appreciate that Dr. Nishank has already got not less than 15 collections and selections of his stories published. Some of these have been translated into Telugu, Tamil, Punjabi and English, etc. The Uttarakhand region is all-pervading in these stories but these stories have a global outlook and perspective as they delineate human nature in all its diversities. 'Man' is the centre of his stories and this man is a universal man. If he celebrates life in *Vah Zindagi* (What a Wonderful Life!), he shares the tragedy and tumult in selections such as *Parlay ke Beech* (Amidst the Great- Food) and *Uttarakhand Tragedy*. He becomes a motivational speaker and consultant when he presents the life-stories of Swami Vivekananda, Vajpayee and A.P.J. Abdul Kalam. Most of the time the reader finds himself immersed and absorbed in the theme of the story and grasps the message in such a way that he himself is not able to express himself.

Any creation is the result of a specific process. Often the question of process is overlooked while evaluating a story. Even the critics deem it a futile exercise and consider the merits and demerits of the product and overlook the process because that is what is in front of us and our immediate purpose is that. The process is behind the creation and only the creator can shed light on it. Moreover, the creative experience of one writer is generally different from the creative experience of another because even though they are contemporaries, they are different. The life-process and consciousness of two different writers is bound to be different. Nishank's stories are realistic in terms of theme, purpose and empathy and are liked by readers as the stories take references from life and the genuineness with which the writer goes forward in his narrative is felt by the readers. He makes the portrayal of the characters, taken from middle-class and lower-middle class of a far-off region, life-like and real.

In the name of reality, some writers think that they can find reality somewhere else, beyond their vicinity and experience. Their novels and short stories thus created from somebody else's reality and experience lack the feeling of attachment and the reader finds such attempts as mere attempts. Take another facet of Dr. Nishank's art of story-telling. When I tried to equate his roving eye with the wandering mirror of Upendra Nath '*Ashk*', I got some proof to prove my point. He has been an active social worker and political face—even a minister and Chief Minister—and was instrumental in guiding his team from the frontline during man-made and natural disasters. *Kedarnath Aapda ki Sachchi Kahaniyan* is based on the Kedarnaath disaster. In these stories, his journalistic flavour and fervour come to the fore. The stories in this collection are woven around some of the true incidents and show not only the nature in tooth and claw but present the human nature at its best. The true shade of humanity had also appeared after the great disaster. Dr. Nishank says: "I saw this disaster very closely. I would have been the first person to reach there soon after the disaster in Kedarnath. The Prime Minister of the country and the then Chief Minister of the state were informed about the casualties of thousands of people. I have seen with my own eyes the sight which a person cannot imagine in a dream. All the things that I saw there and went to meet people have made the same events the subject of the stories in this book."[5]

In a way, these are true stories of the Kedarnath disaster. Even in the very first story '*Aur Mein Kuch na Kar Saka,* one can get a glimpse of the sensitivity of the narrator. The main character of the story is 'Dabboo', a horse. This story reminds us of two other well-known stories—one is Premchand's *Do Bailon ki Katha* and the other is Sudershan's *Haar ki Jeet*:

> वह सिर्फ घोड़ा नहीं था, बल्कि इस परिवार का एक सदस्य ही था। दयाल उसे अपना बेटा मानता था। आखिर उसकी मेहनत से ही तो दयाल का घर-परिवार चलता था। संवेदनाएँ उसमें कूट-कूटकर भरी थीं, सिर्फ आवाज ही नहीं है उसके अंदर। यात्रा सीजन में दोनों खूब मेहनत करते।[6]
> (It was not only a horse but also a member of the family. Dayal treated him as a member of his family. After all, the entire family depended on his toil and hard work. He was the solitary bread-earner. He had no human voice but the milk of humanity was there in his veins. During the *yatra*-season, both used to work very hard.)

Story-telling Technique

Nishank's story-telling technique is unpretentious with a natural element of humour about it. It focuses on ordinary people, reminding the reader of next-door neighbours, cousins and the like, thereby providing a greater ability to relate to the topic. He also employs the use of nuanced dialogic prose with a gentle use of the words spoken in the region, based on the nature of his characters. When I went through a selection of

21 stories available in English, I could feel as if I was reading R.K. Narayan of *Malgudi Days* fame. I am not sure if these stories are written in English or are translated but I am sure that the stories have the same captivating feeling as his novels. Most of the stories are short and can be read within a few minutes. His attitude, coupled with his perception of life, provides a unique ability to fuse characters and actions and the ability to use ordinary events to create a connection in the mind of the reader.

Let me take up the first story, 'The Only Wish' of this selection. It has the kind of intimacy we find bewitching and mesmerising. It starts as follows:

> "There was something about the boy that attracted me. His innocent face was compelling me to see him frequently. He carried my suitcase and made his way to the room. "Sir, may I leave?" he asked after providing all the necessary information about the room."[7]
>
> And it ends thus:
>
> "It has been many years now. His innocent face is engraved so deep in my memory that I'm unable to forget."[8]

In between the story is narrated. The story of a boy Vikram is told with such inborn simplicity and concern that the reader will be hooked to it in no time. You will find for yourself that Nishank's stories are not just stories; they are loaded with some inherent message and educate the reader. Many a time, his message is so apparent and clear as if he wishes to write, not for telling a story, but instilling a message into the minds of the reader. Here is a snip from the ending of a story:

> शहर का हर शख्स आज झूठे दिखावे व छलावे में जी रहा है। किसी को किसी से कोई मतलब नहीं। हर कोई अपने स्वार्थों व निजी जिंदगी में इतना खो गया है कि उसे अपने लोगों के बारे में सोचने का भी समय ही नहीं है। संकीर्ण मानसिकता लिये भौतिकवाद के सहारे अनजान मंजिल की तरफ अंधी दौड़ लगाते अपने घर की चारदीवारी तक सिमटे हुए इन लोगों को दूसरे के दु:खों से आखिर क्या सरोकार।[9]

(Today every person in the city lives in false appearances and deception. Nobody has any business with anyone. They are lost in their personal lives and selfish motives that they don't even have time to think about their own people. For these people nothing matters as they are all blindfolded in their narrow walls running about material gains unmindful of others' sufferings and woes.)

I haven't spoiled anything by quoting from the ending. This is not going to spoil your mood. You can still read the story entitled very appropriately as *theeya*.

There has been one of the several trends in Hindi stories from the early days till now that the story-tellers employ no twist and turns and tell the story for the sake of delivering a message. The environment is created with the help of descriptions but these too are kept minimal. The early short-story writers in Hindi, such as Subhadra Kumari Chauhan, Homvati Devi and Shivrani Premchand told the story without any ostentation. Dr. Nishank has a local colour for his background. Like Goura Pant 'Shivani' and Himanshu Joshi, Dr. Nishank uses his upbringing in the Uttarakhand region to his advantage. He has been a keen observer of the lives of the people around him and they provide him plenty of raw material for his stories. He has been presenting the case of those subalterns who have no voice or are not being heard. Their minuscule desires, their pithy demands and their happy lives amidst all the pains are portrayed and displayed in an unpretentious manner by Dr. Nishank through his stories.

सच ही तो कह रहा था वह ! यदि गरीब भूखे पेट रामदेई और उसके बच्चों की तरह इसी प्रकार हटते रहे, तो एक न एक दिन गरीबी तो सदा के लिए अपने आप ही हट जाएगी न।[10]

(Indeed! He was telling the truth. If the poor half-fed like Ramdei and her children are displaced like this, that day is not far when the poverty will be out of sight without any effort.)

Nashank's stories are successful and are being read as he possesses what Fitzgerald calls the 'honesty of imagination'. He doesn't create myths but his 'monomyths' (the protagonist's small journey in life) immerse the readers in the story. He is not 'I' in the story but the way he tells the story is intimate and personal.

Dr. Nishank's writing style can be compared to that of William Faulkner as both draw upon ordinary life and rely on humane noble characters. Dr. Nishank is able to bring compassionate humanism in his short stories as Premchand was able to bring out the element of change of heart. The pen used by Dr. Nishank is not mightier than the sword but milder than the milk of benevolence. He does not write stories as an unattached journalist but writes the actual feelings of the men in the street. A short-story '*Raddivala*' is a very short-story indeed! The protagonist is a person who collects and resells old books and newspapers. He is an ordinary man of the street. The narrator is a gentleman and the protagonist visits him on and off. They sometimes discuss certain topics of mutual interest. This person is also familiar with the narrator's bent of mind. That is the reason that one day he tells him, "आपकी हिंदी साहित्य में रुचि है न, एक बहुत बढ़िया किताब हाथ लगी है। आप कहें तो आपको पढ़ने के लिए दे दूँ।"[11]

> (You have interest in Hindi literature, I have got a very good book. If you wish, I shall give it to you to read.)

That novel was *Gunahon ka Devta* by Dharmveer Bharati. This marks the beginning of their friendship. It shows that the waste-paper *wallah* is an educated man with remarkable literary sensibilities. As soon as he gets a good book, he gives it to him. The climax of the story is really fantastic. The narrator's daughter Meghna passes engineering and MBA examinations. She is a very talented and independent girl. Her parents want to know if she is in love with anyone. Meghna is very forthcoming and tells her parents that she has already selected a gentleman of a very high character to be her life-partner. He is an IAS officer posted as Collector in an adjoining state. The beauty of the story is that in the end, the Collector is found to be the son of the same *raddiwallah*.

I hope you will consider it worth your time to read the rest of the story. I haven't spoiled anything by quoting from the beginning. Of course, these are mere translations. Reading in the original Hindi would be something else entirely.

It is widely said and believed that stories are scattered around us and an expert story-teller needn't struggle to get stories as his sharp eyes and sensitive mind watch the story unfold in every individual he sees. Even the tiny spark tells him a story. Dr. Nishank has that sharp vision with which he is able to perceive stories and his stories become a bold statement on the people living the life of the oppressed and marginalised. He creates the story through the characters and events, about poverty and meagreness, relationships and break-up, family and filial passion and above all, irony of the whole life lived so meaningfully but meaninglessly. Thomas Hardy, the great novelist, finds happiness an occasional episode in the general drama of pain, while Dr. Nishank doesn't utter any such words but his characters speak for him. In *Eik thi Juhi*, we find these prophetic lines:

> ज्यादा मत सोच इस बारे में। बस अब तो यही सोच कि तेरे कारण तेरे परिवार की दशा सुधर रही है। कितना पुण्य का काम कर रही है तू अपने घर की पाँच जिंदगियों को बचाकर।[12]
>
> (Don't think much about it. Now think only this much; because of you the condition of your family is getting improved. You are doing a great job by saving the five lives of your family.)

There is no doubt that all the challenges as a person I faced have been mine and the life lived by Dr. Nishank is his. You and I and the author and even others lead their own respective lives under their respective circumstances. What Om Prakash Valmiki writes in the novel *Jhuthan* are his experiences and what Dr. Nishank writes in his novels and stories are his challenges and expereinces. His life is his brilliant story as yours. His fascination for his is comparable with an average reader's. In other words, our private experiences contain enough material to be qualified as collective experiences. This is the reason I write this book and you read it.

To cut the long story short, as the title of this chapter indicates too, the short stories penned by Dr. Ramesh Pokhriyal 'Nishank' penetrate the spirit of those who have a pulsating heart and awakened soul. If one comes here for embalming one's tormenting state to receive the soothing effect, one will not be disheartened and dismayed. Let me cite Dr. Nishank and conclude:

> इसी धड़कन में मेरे अंदर आम आदमी की व्यथा-कथा से जुड़ने की छटपटाहट और उसकी आवाज बनने की अकुलाहट पैदा की। उसके अस्तित्व ही नहीं, अस्मिता की लड़ाई भी लड़ने का जोश भरा है। आत्मीय, सामाजिक रिश्ते व दायरों से लेकर परिवेश के लिए संवेदना जगाई है। यही पीड़ा समय-समय पर मेरी कहानियों में अभिव्यक्त भी होती आई है।

□

8

Inspired and Inspiring Mode

A profusion of arguments!
The *Smritis* differ among themselves.
No one's opinion is final or conclusive
The essence of *dharma* is hidden and elusive.
The right path is the path followed by great men.*

We have many sacred books (*Srutis*, *Smritis*, *Itihas*, *Puranas*, *Agamas*, and *Darshanas*) and a host of known and unknown writers who have been inspiring us. The poets-*rishis*-philosophers have been there since the haze of antiquity. We have always been in an inspired and inspiring mode. As Swami Vivekananda says that to the Westerners, their religious books have been inspired while with us, our books have been expired; breath-like they came, the breath of God, out of the hearts of sages they sprang, the *mantra-drashtas*. Our youth takes inspiration from anywhere and everywhere and instinctively reveres those who inspire.

Dr. Ramesh Pokhriyal 'Nishank' has not only been writing poems, stories and novels but also self-help books and biographies of great men. His books on Indian culture and way of life are also noteworthy in this regard where he aims at his readers' attention for their own good and betterment. Whatever Dr. Nishank has learnt from life till date, he wants to pen his experiences for the benefit of others. He wants his readers to have a more successful lifestyle:

> *"What is needed to succeed in life—Fate or hard work? The answer to this question would decide the journey of success. Many a time, we see some successful person and say, "That person is so lucky! I wish I were him!"*[1]

His aim is to provide his readers with a slice of his inspiring life, full of ups and downs. The vicissitudes of his life may be inspiring for many in the way he himself got inspired by great men, such as Swami Vivekananda, Abdul Kalam and Atal Bihari Vajpayee and Yogiraj Arvind.

He is enamoured with India, Indian culture and the country's rich and varied heritage. As a motivational speaker and writer, Dr. Nishank has been providing his readers values and insights about Bharart Mata and nationalism. The following words will indicate his ideas and ideals: "Indian culture is like a large banyan tree. It teaches how to live life with an ideal viewpoint and how to live it artfully. People of many castes, religions and communities reside in this vast ocean like world."[2]

Swami Vivekananda

There is no doubt that the life and teachings of Swami Vivekananda have been a great influence on Dr. Nishank's life and works. Vivekananda's idealism and ideals are found in many of the characters presented by Dr. Nishank. Vivekananda's life and mission are also portrayed and presented in the books on him. On 25th October, 2019, Dr. Ramesh Pokhriyal 'Nishank' tweeted, "Swami Vivekanandaji was a prolific thinker, great orator and one of the most celebrated spiritual leaders of India." According to him, education must provide 'life-building, man-making and character-building ideas to transform learners into intellectual beings. *Himalaya mein Vivekananda* (2019), a book by Dr. Nishank, became so popular that its English edition was printed in no time. I could find more books on him by Dr. Nishank and was also delighted to look at the translations in some regional languages also. Let me cite an extract from the English translation of the above-mentioned book:

"Swami Vivekananda, the symbolic figure of modern India, discovered his ethereal self with renewed energy and brilliance with *Shaktipunj* found in this ancient abode of gods and saints. He acquired his plenary knowledge of the Hindu philosophy, human life, culture and civilisation, science, and history from the Uttarakhand Himalayas. The young monk, Narendra, travelled everywhere in the Himalayas in Uttarakhand for answers to his questions and realised the infinitesimal atomic knowledge from within the natural magnificence in a place Kakrighat, near Almora."[3]

Atal Bihari Vajpayee

"You stop anything but never stop writing" was the sound advice given to Dr. Nishank by Atal Bihari Vajpayee, former Prime Minister. Dr. Nishank has more to say about Atalji beyond the 450-page book titled *Yug Purush, Bharat Ratna, Atalji* (2017) which is worth reading. Dr. Nishank very often finds in Atalji a political pandit who inspired him to work for the masses through politics. For Dr. Nishank, Atalji has been a torch-bearer and a pathfinder. Reading the preface of the book, *Mere Atal Jee* is an exhilarating experience. It not only tells us about Atalji but also about Dr. Nishank. The confluence of 'politics and poetry' is palpable on every page of the book.

भारतीय संस्कृति के पुरोधा, राजनीति में देदीप्यमान सितारा, सरल संवेदनशील, सहृदय व्यक्तित्व, जिसने अपना सर्वस्व माँ भारती को अर्पण किया, ऐसे युगपुरुष के विषय में लिखना मेरे लिए गौरव का विषय है। भारतीय राजनीति के शिखर-पुरुष अजातशत्रु एवं पूर्व प्रधानमंत्री भारत रत्न श्री अटल बिहारी वाजपेयी भारत के ऐसे दुर्लभ नेताओं में एक हैं जिनकी सर्वत्र स्वीकार्यता रही और इसी कारण उन्हें जननायक की छवि प्राप्त हुई है। वे ऐसे नेता हैं जिनकी स्वीकार्यता जाति, धर्म, संप्रदाय, पार्टी, और दल की विचारधारा से हटकर न सिर्फ भारत अपितु संपूर्ण विश्व के हर वर्ग और हर उम्र के जनमानस में है।

(It is a matter of great pride for me to write about such an illustrious man, a pioneer of Indian culture, a brilliant star in politics, and a simple sensitive and gentle person who offered his best to Mother India. He is aptly called 'Ajatshatru', one who has no enemy. The pinnacle of Indian politics, former Prime Minister of India, Bharat Ratna (a jewel of India), Shri Atal Bihari Vajpayee is one of the rare leaders of India who has been universally accepted and for this reason he has got the sobriquet of Jannayak. He is a leader whose acceptance remains unassailed not only in India but also in the people of all classes and all ages in the entire world irrespective of caste, religion, sect, party, and party ideology.)

A.P.J. Abdul Kalam

For Indians, the name of Dr. A.P.J. Abdul Kalam, the 'people's President', needs no introduction. He has been a role-model for many and it is no surprise that Dr. Nishank too finds in him an icon worth emulating. He had the golden opportunities to meet him a number of times and interact with him which motivated him to pen down a book on Dr. Kalam's life experiences and his management skills. *Dreams that Don't Let You Sleep* (2016) is a self-help book which motivates the generations now and yet to come. Dr. Kalam's following words can take the readers towards his philosophy of life: "What actions are most excellent? To gladden the heart of a human being, to feed the hungry, to help the afflicted, to lighten the sorrow of the sorrowful, and to remove the sufferings of injured..."[4]

I must fail in my duty if I don't tell you that this book is not based on mere dry facts about Dr. Kalam but the aim throughout is to enrich the reader with the experiences Dr. Nishank had about Dr. Kalam. The anecdotal narration (some treasured moments with Kalam) captures our attention and the reader, who reads such books with a pencil in hand, will surely jot down the jewels scattered here and there.

After the book release ceremony, Dr. Kalam opened a folded page of my book and recited a few words from it in his 'not so fluent' Hindi:

Abhi bhi hai jung jaari, vedna soyi nahi hai
Manujta hogi dhara par, samvedna khoi nahin hai
Keh raha hun ea watan, tujse bada koi nahi hai.

While reciting the last two verses from the poem ('Nothing is bigger and dearer than you, my beloved nation), Dr. Kalam got emotional. I could gauge the patriotric spirit of this man through his words and eyes while reciting these lines.[5]

Pandit Deendayal Upadhyaya

Pt. Deendayal Upadhyaya (1916-1968) was an Indian politician and thinker associated with the Rastriya Swayamsevak Sangh (RSS) and the forerunner of Bharatiya Jananta Party (BJP). Vinayak Damodar Savarkar (1883-1966) gave us the concept of Hindutva to describe the quality of being a Hindu in ethnic, political and cultural terms. M.S. Golwarkar (1906-1973), who headed the Rashtriya Swayamsevak Sangh (RSS) for three decades (1940-1973), taught us about 'cultural nationalism'. Like Veer Savarkar and Guruji M.S. Golwalkar, Deendayal Upadhyaya worked to decolonise Indian political thought. He was respected across the party. Even a veteran Congressman of Uttar Pradesh, Sampurnanand, wrote in the preface of Upadhyaya's *Political Diary*, describing him as "one of the most notable political leaders of our time." These stalwarts and several others of their ilk provide Dr. Nishank the ideological insights into nationhood, Hinduism and cultural humanism.

Dr. Ramesh Pokhriyal 'Nishank' wrote a book on him to let his readers know about his philosophy and work. The book in Hindi not only presents Pt. Deendayal Upadhyaya's philosophy of 'integral humanism' but also his ideology. When you look at the foreword of the book, you can also find the purpose and intent of the book as follows:

> आज जरूरत उनका सच्चा उत्तराधिकारी बनकर उनका ऋण चुकाने की है, उनके खून-पसीने की एक-एक बूँद को माथे का चंदन बनाकर 'ध्येय पथ' पर आगे बढ़ने की है, उनके भारतीय पुनर्निर्माण के सपने को साकार करने की है। आइए, हम सब मिलकर आज उनकी पावन जन्म शताब्दी पर अंतर्मन से यह संकल्प लें और अतीत के गौरवशाली भारत की नींव पर 'आधुनिकतम भारत का भव्य भवन खड़ा करने को तन-मन से जुट जाएँ।[6]
> (Today the need of the hour is to be his true heir, to repay his debt, to transform every drop of his blood and sweat into sandal on our forehead, to realise his dream of India's reconstruction. Come, let us all together today take this pledge from the core of our hearts on the eve of his birth centenary to get ready to build a grand edifice of 'modern India' on the foundation of our great glorious past.)

Human Values

If literature reflects social realities, then it has to embody human values. If it embodies human values, naturally its study will eventually leave impressions on its readers. One of the ways in which literature might embody and promote values is to see if it helps refine our ethical reflections and inform our moral choices. The case of the benevolent lie in Kant (is it right to lie to a murderer if it will save a life?) and Bernard William's story about a man who has the opportunity to save lives if he agrees to kill one person are often cited in the West to pinpoint the dilemma of value judgement. In times of self-centredness, greed, corruption, political scandals and materialism, the protagonist's values stand as a cornerstone of fairness, honesty and justice—values that are closely associated with but not always found in our society. When the world is in a process of transition and the 'time is out of joint', it is better to follow Shakespeare of 1599 who asked one of his characters of the play *Hamlet* to speak, 'more matter, with less art.' It is admitted that in imbibing its values, which it emphasises by showing the debasement of those values, we become better persons and that state of being a better person needs to be transformed into something concrete and practical.

Dr. Nishank has equated value with culture when he discusses the role of Indian culture in propagating human values through literature:

> "Actually the literal meaning of culture is 'value', the effort of giving a cultural form to some object. Culture is surely the soul of a nature and the background for class, but also a symbol of their inner philosophy and spiritual elevation. It gives rise to these values, in which the delicate elements of life are present."[7]

Life Values

When I started writing these lines, one of his ardent readers informed me that Nishank's text can be primarily read with a view to knowing underlying values, universal as well as local. Dr. Nishank is a preacher of human values and he has been writing to educate the reader in those age-old values on which the edifice of Indian culture resides. Yes, it is there to see but let me go beyond this surmise. First of all, I am going to ask my reader to recollect what these different terms mean. Are they similar or different?

It was Paul Tillich, who once said that our knowledge of values is identical with the knowledge of man. Since men differ, values also differ. Many scholars tried to pinpoint certain universal values as the values can be greatly influenced by local, regional and national flavour. *Aatmanah pratikulani paresham na samachret* (Do unto others as you would have others do unto you) can be a universal human value. Similarly, love in different forms is universal. On the other hand, many Western anthropologists have taken an anti-universalist position also. They say that values can't be universal, for example, 'modesty' can be an Indian life-value but there are cultures in which modesty has a limit. Some psychologists call values as unreal, for example, truth can be a universal value but defining truth is as difficult as defining democracy. Gandhi too proposed some values as universal. He said that non-violence is a universal value as all people have a reason to value non-violence.

Jeevan Mulya

Dr. Yogendra Nath Sharma 'Arun' wrote a book titled *Kathakar Nishank ke Upanyasoon Mein Jeevan Mulya*. The erudite author tried to look at 10 of his novels with a view to underlining life values so that the novelist's readers get an insight into Nishank's range and profound ideals that are free from so-called ideology. Dr. Arun's hypothesis in this book has been as follows:

> मेरा स्पष्ट मानना है कि जीवन–मूल्यों के सार्थक और सजीव चित्रण से ही साहित्यकार की रचना कालजयी और दीर्घजीवी हो पाती है।[7]
> (I obviously believe that it is only through a meaningful and lively depiction of life values that a writer's work can be established, sustained and long-lived.)

'Only through a meaningful and lively depiction' is the phrase used by Dr. Arun. He enumerates some of the values as follows: renunciation, devotion, tolerance, mutual cooperation, patriotism, dutifulness, etc. Dr. Yogendra Nath Sharma 'Arun' presents this book in the format of a thesis and academic discourse. Wisdom and knowledge coupled with keen observation is so widespread throughout the book that the reader will become speechless and overawed with gratitude. I have neither wisdom nor a sense of proportion. That is why I am neither going to tell you what you can get there nor am I in a mood to reinvent the wheel. My humble submission is to explore certain universal values in these novels. My aim is very modest and indicative only. I have no readymade conclusion also to offer to my readers. You are free to come to a conclusion of your own.

> मेरा तो निष्कर्ष यही है कि कथाकार के रूप में डॉ. रमेश पोखरियाल 'निशंक' निश्चय ही जीवन–मूल्यों को साथ लेकर चले हैं और उच्चतर

जीवन-मूल्यों, जैसे—त्याग, समर्पण, सहिष्णुता, सहयोग, राष्ट्रप्रेम, कर्तव्यबोध, पारस्परिक सहयोग, एवं वैयक्तिक निष्ठा आदि का सजीव चित्रण उनके सभी उपन्यासों में हुआ है।[8]

(My conclusion is that as a narrator, Dr. Ramesh Pokhriyal 'Nishank' has definitely carried the values of life and of higher values such as renunciation, dedication, tolerance, cooperation, national pride, sense of duty, mutual support and personal loyalty, etc. through the depiction of these in his novels and short stories.)

The critic in him has selected the following 10 novels of Dr. Nishank and after a thorough reading of each novel, it was found that the novels have the life values which can be presented as follows:

1. A symbol of strong expression of socio-cultural life values. —*Beera*
2. The mirror of expression of national and human values. —*Major Nirala*
3. A mirror of the strong expression of life values of Uttarakhand society. —*Pahad se Uncha.*

   A living mirror of poignant feelings and ecstatic life values. —*Apna Paraya.*
4. An expression of woman's beauty, courage, dedication, and lofty values. —*Pallavi.*
5. The victory over truth and justice over injustice and untruth, good over evil. —*Pratigya*
6. Swinging between the ideal and reality. —Chut gaya Padav.
7. Lively witness of the value of the dignity of womanhood. —*Nishant*
8. Strong expression against negativity in life. —*Krataghnn.*
9. Depicting the shattered life values of the society. —*Bhagonvali.*

After citing scholars, both Indian and Western, Dr. Arun concludes:

> जीवन-मूल्य यदि वास्तव में जीवन-मूल्य हैं तो उन्हें प्राचीनता और नवीनता की सीमाओं में बाँधा ही नहीं जा सकता, बल्कि जीवन-मूल्य तो मानव जीवन की तरह ही शाश्वत और स्थायी होते हैं। जीवन-मूल्यों के निर्धारण में समाज, धर्म, दर्शन, संस्कृति, साहित्य, अर्थनीति, राजनीति की ही तरह विज्ञान की भी महत्त्वपूर्ण भूमिका रहती है। जीवन-मूल्यों के अभाव में कोई मानव या उसका समाज प्रगति अथवा उसका विकास नहीं कर सकता। यह युग सत्य है, जिसे प्रत्येक युग के चिंतकों ने स्वीकार किया है।[9]
>
> (If the values of life are really life values, they can't be restricted by the boundaries of antiquity and newness, but the values of life are eternal and permanent like human life. Society, religion, philosophy, culture, literature, economics, politics, science, also plays an important role in determining the values of life. In the absence of life-values, no human being or his society can progress or develop. This is an absolute truth accepted by the thinkers of every era.)

In a very confident and scholarly fashion Dr. Arun connects literature with life values so that their interdependence is ascertained:

> जीवन-मूल्यों की यथार्थ अभिव्यक्ति साहित्य की प्राण-शक्ति कही जा सकती है।
>
> (The true expression of life values can be called the life-force of literature.)

It has been reiterated by many scholars that Dr. Nishank is a novelist who is chiefly interested in human values. His insistence on basic human values and human rights takes him to create characters who are epitomes of Indian values. For instance, in the novel, *Pallavi,* the protagonist Dhruv is not only a mouthpiece of the novelist, but also a harbinger of noble virtues and values. Like the novelist, he is also a poet and sings well. Thus, as a novelist, Dr. Nishank plays a vital role in reforming and reconstructing the society. He knows his people and their conditions well and is able to inspire them to come out of their problematic and tough lives. He is deeply pained to see the misery of the old, the women and the infirm. He always takes sides with the wretched of the Earth that have been pushed out of the main stream.

Nishank's stories are not rooted in the themes related to human psyche and can be at times too simplistic in tone and tenor. However, these stories fulfil a double function. For Dr. Nishank, they are a way of self-expression in the service of the cause of the nation-building and for the readers, they are a way of constructing meaning and value. This is the reason that at first glance a critic and a reader finds in him a person who is there to impart life values and his fiction is taken as lessons in human values. A close reading of the stories will reveal that the stories are not meant for arm-chair readers; they are also above the politics of the coffee-table. Like the characters in the stories, these are vibrant with life.

Universal Values

While moving the Central Sanskrit Universities Bill, 2019 on 12th December, 2019, Dr. Ramesh Pokhriyal Nishank recited the following Sanskrit *shlokas*:

एतद्देशप्रसूतस्यसकाशादग्रजन्मनः।
स्वंस्वंचरित्रंशिक्षेरन, पृथिव्यांसर्वमानवः।

(All men on the earth may learn their respective duties from the Brāhmaa born in these countries.)

अयंनिजः परोवेतिगणनालघुचेतसाम।
उदारचरितानामतुवसुधैवकुटुम्बकम॥

(He is mine, he is another, not mine—such are the thoughts of narrow-minded people. For the noble minded the whole world is a family.)

सर्वेभवन्तुसुखिन:सर्वेसन्तुनिरामया:।
सर्वेभद्राणिपश्यन्तुमाकश्चिद्दु:खभाग्भवेत्॥

(May all be very happy and free from all diseases!
May all perceive goodness and none suffer from any grief.)

These *shlokas* can very clearly show anyone the way Dr. Nishank looks at the universal values. His value system primarily rests on the scriptures and Indian cultural tradition. In March, during the debate on the Motion of Thanks on the President's Address, he recited the following stanza of one of his poems:

तुम क्या जानो आजादी क्या होती है,
तुम्हें मुफ्त में मिली है, न कोई कीमत चुकाई है।
(What do you know about freedom?
You have got it for free, you didn't have to pay for it.)

He then followed up with these lines to signal the nation's firm resolution about the issue at hand then:

अब कोई सपना मत देखो कि भूमि बाँट ली जाएगी।
अब जो देश बाँटने की माँग करेगा, उसकी जीभ काट दी जाएगी।
अब तो सीमा पार हो गई सहते-सहते सहने की,
इसलिए जरूरत पड़ती है अब चिल्ला-चिल्लाकर कहने की
कि जिसे मेरे देश से प्यार नहीं, उसे भारत में रहने का कोई अधिकार नहीं।

(Now don't dream about this land being divided.
If you demand a division of the land, your tongue will be cut.
Now we crossed all the limits of the tolerance
That is why we need to should and express ourselves.
Whoever doesn't love my country India?
Has no right to live here.)

Universal values are those that are not limited to a particular region. They cut across national, ethnic, religious and linguistic boundaries. They are common to all states. They may not be eternal but they are durable and their longevity is beyond doubt. Universal values integrate the broad vision of the good life. Needless to say that Dr. Nishank's universalism goes through the portals of national pride. A regional, national and international reading of Dr. Nishank's text will reveal that his characters are regional, but their concerns are endowed with universal values. When a character in Nishank's novel asks for it, for example, in the novel *Pahad se Uncha*, Shankar Dutt and his son-in-law Dr. Mohan, both live for others. He is the embodiment of those universal values that are democratic and full of piety. Dr. Mohan is a shadow of Dr. A.P.J. Abdul Kalam.

□

9
The End for the Beginning

Life has no end in the way our visual field has no limit.
—Ludwig Wittgenstein

We all know what the word 'end' ('closure' and 'finis' are the other two loaded meta-textual terms) indicates. We cannot do without the notion of end as the goal or purpose (or, in its Greek form, *telos*). But we generally fail to understand that it is a new beginning too. Joseph Conrad was often unable to 'finis' his novels but this became his remarkable quality and identification. In Hindi, there is a word *upsamhar* and the use of a prefix before the word *samhar* denotes that it is not the 'complete end'. In *Little Gidding* (1942), T.S. Eliot writes:

To make an end is to make a beginning.
The end is where we start from.

And our great Goswami Tulsidas in the *Ramayana* says:

नहिं तव आदि मध्य अवसाना।
अमित प्रभाव वेद नहीं जाना॥

(Your beginning, middle and end are not known. Even the *Vedas* don't know your real and great clout and worth.)

There is a Polish poem *The End and the Beginning*, by Wisława Szymborska in which she says there is always something better in the *end*. The *end* of harsh times will always bring a *new beginning*. British Prime Minister

Winston Churchill, who received the Nobel Prize in literature, proclaimed in 1942 as follows:

> "Now this is not the end. It is not even the beginning of the end. But it is, perhaps, the end of the beginning."

Many readers say that they could hardly find any book other than *The Holy Bible* which begins with a proper beginning (In the beginning...) and a proper vision of the end ('Even so, come, Jesus'). Don't you remember how our mythological Kansa got confused when Sage Narada arrived with a lotus flower to tell him that no petal of the flower was the last/first one? The great sage Narada baffled him by giving an illustration. He picked the flower and asked Kansa which one was the first petal and which was the last. He made the evil presence trust that any child of Devaki could be the eighth child. Kansa thought that it was better than before to execute every child of Devaki and not to take a risk in this regard.

The physician Alkmeon observed, with Aristotle's approval, that men die because they cannot join the beginning and the end. Man is mortal but doesn't want to accept the fact. Ibn Kathir (1300-1373), in a 14-volume classic text on Sunni Islamic history, *The Beginning and the End* says that both are one and the same. One of the attractions of literature is that it provides an outlet to expression for life and death, both. Surya Kant Tripathi 'Nirala' in one of the poems indicates: अभी न होगा मेरा अंत। (I will not come to an end so soon).

The final stanza of a poem or a novel or a short story is not the desirable end in the real sense of the term. In the same way, the last chapter of a book—this book—is also not the last one. It is the beginning of our contemplation and foundation of critical appreciation of the text and a solid ground for reading and rereading of Dr. Nishank's text. For some readers, it is going to be the beginning of a memorable relationship with him. The end, if there is any, in a literary text, then it must be the conclusion as if the goal or the purpose of the text is attained by the author and the reader as well. Neither is true. When the second and subsequent editions of the book appear, the author is at liberty to change the text as he likes. Derrida says, "Plenitude is the end (the goal), but were it is attained; it would be the end (death).:[1] Therefore, I would like to end this chapter in an unconventional way. No end, but beginning.

We are going to look to the end to provide answers to questions that the entire text of the book has put forward. In order to make sense of our lives we need to find some 'consonance' between the beginning, the middle and the end. We can't totally rely on authors and poets to help us make sense of our lives. There are many others, such as philosophers and gurus, who are also there to help us. But the poets and the authors present a mirror of society in which they live and it is on us to make use of it accordingly. We read Dr. Nishank for making sense of our lives as what he is offering is a 'slice of life'. It will be worthwhile to see in Dr. Nishank's fiction a concord of imaginatively recorded past and imaginatively predicted future, achieved on behalf of the readers, who remain 'in the middest.'[2]

The Beginning

Dr. Nishank is an author with a purpose. In this chapter we discuss the end and there is no doubt that there must have been a beginning, if there is an end. Ruminating on the very nature of a story's start, one of the greatest novelists of all time, Graham Greene comments as follows: "A story has no beginning or end; arbitrarily one chooses that moment of experience from which to look back or from which to look ahead." In Hindi, Agyeya's novel, *Shekhar: Eik Jeevani* starts from the end. Let me look at the novel, *Nishant*. The first few lines of the novel present the setting and begin as follows:

> तेज हवा के झोंके के साथ खिड़की के पट जोर की आवाज के साथ खुल गए तो कमरे में बेचैनी से टहलती मीताली ने शॉल कसकर लपेट

> लिया। खिड़की को बंद करने के लिए मीताली ज्यों ही उधर बढ़ी इतने में आसमान में जोर की गर्जना हुई और बिजली गुल हो गई। 'उफ्फ! आज तो लगता है भीषण तूफान आएगा।' मीताली ने मन-ही-मन सोचा और खिड़की बंद कर ली।[3]
>
> (With a gust of strong wind, the doors of the window opened with a loud thud. Mitali strolling with restiveness in[3] the room wrapped the shawl tightly. As soon as Mithali grew there to close the window, there was a loud roar in the sky and lightning went on. Oops! Today there seems to be a severe storm, Mitali thought and closed the window.)

This is the beginning of a novel and there is no novelty in this beginning. In fact, it is a usual beginning of the novel. Does life begin like that? This is no beginning or end here as the birth is the beginning and the death is the end in our lives. This is the beginning in the middle—*in medias res*—and almost all novels and stories begin from the middle. It seems as if the ancient poet Homer laid down a rule for his successors when he began his epic by plunging *in medias res*, 'into the midst of things'. Poets and novelists freely begin their stories wherever they like. Here is the middle of life in which Mitali and Nishant are leading a contented life. In chapter two of the novel, the story begins in a flashback mode.

When the reader finishes this back and forth exercise and reaches the end, s/he finds that the end is the same as the beginning of the novel once again. Once we read it together with the end or read it from beginning to the end, we understand the story. Look at the last lines intently:

> कर्नल की आवाज सुन कर मीताली और निशांत तुरंत एक-दूसरे से अलग होकर अपनी झेंप मिटाते सहज होने का प्रयास करते हुए बाहर बरामदे में आ चुके थे। मिलन की वास्तविक खुशी आज उनके चेहरे पर साफ पढ़ी और महसूस की जा रही थी।[4]

> (Hearing the voice of the Colonel, Mitali and Nishant immediately broke apart and tried to be comfortable wiping away their blush and came out to the verandah. The real happiness of Milan was clearly read and felt on his face today.)

The End

Frank Karmode, in his path-breaking book, *The Sense of an Ending* (1967), provides a fascinating outline of a theory of fiction where he says that we all share some fiction and it is human nature to search for some coherent patterns in our lives. Our need for ends is satisfied by reading 'the end' in literature. Emile Zola formulates the theory of pure realism and says that the novelist is but a recorder who is forbidden to judge and conclude. A novelist is merely an agent of verisimilitude. Dr. Nishank has understood these viewpoints very well. Here is a slice from the ending of a story by Dr. Nishank:

> शहर का हर शख्स आज झूठे दिखावे व छलावे में जी रहा है। किसी को किसी से कोई मतलब नहीं। हर कोई अपने स्वार्थों व निजी जिंदगी में इतना खो गया है कि उसे अपने लोगों के बारे में सोचने का भी समय ही नहीं है। संकीर्ण मानसिकता लिये भौतिकवाद के सहारे अनजान मंजिल की तरफ अंधी दौड़ लगाते अपने घर की चारदीवारी तक सिमटे हुए इन लोगों को दूसरे के दु:खों से आखिर क्या सरोकार।[5]
>
> (Today every person in the city lives in false appearances and deception. Nobody has any business with anyone. They are lost in their personal lives and selfish motives that they don't even have time to think about their own people. For these people nothing matters as they are all blindfolded in their narrow walls running about material gains, unmindful of others' sufferings and woes.)

Dr. Nishank is commenting as a preacher and giving his expert advice to the readers as if it was not enough to let the characters speak for themselves. You can pick up any story or novel to substantiate this claim. Let us take up a short story. The title of the story attracts our attention. It is *Antheen* (endless):

> और इसी घबराहट में लाला को आजकल फिर ऐसे कर्जदार की तलाश है, जहाँ कोई बेटी हो और लाला बाप-बेटी दोनों का उद्धार कर सके। झुमकी की हालत दिन-प्रति-दिन बिगड़ती जा रही है और उसी गति से लुभाया का बोझ भी।[6]
>
> (And with the same fright, nowadays Lala is looking for such a borrower where there is a father and his daughter and Lala can save and protect both of them. The condition of Jhumki is getting worse day by day and the burden of Lubhaya is also at the same pace.)

The Beginning and the End

Apna Paraya (2015) is a novel based on social realities of life. In a single sentence, the novelist is able to capture the complete life cycle of the protagonist. The novel has intertwined two stories into one. There is a story of Suresh and Laxmi and another one is of Rahul-Anita and Rashmi. Laxmi is the glue with which the characters are joined. She stands for womanhood and gives the novel a feminist look. The novelist is also trying to portray the lives of the middle-class people who have their own economic and social worries, problems of relationships and traditional values. Look at the ultimate final sentence of the novel:

> जीवन का एक अध्याय समाप्त हुआ, लेकिन राहुल के जीवन में माँ की अंतिम इच्छा के रूप में एक नया अध्याय आरंभ होनेवाला था।[7]
>
> (One chapter of life was over, but in Rahul's life a new chapter was going to start as the last will of his dear departed mother.)

Not in stories but very often in the novels we find the novelist trying to reach a point (climax) and call it a day. He wants to bid farewell to his readers who have been in the journey along with him for so long. It is a very sad decision but is a must too. Even the greatest epics are found to be dragging the narration or tend to start preaching. *Ramcharitmanas* has seven chapters but the seventh one is largely didactic and too long to sustain the interest. As a narrator and story-teller, Dr. Nishank brings forth the sordid tales of the marginalised and oppressed, allowing the reader the freedom to imagine the end and beyond it. The tale is presented as a take-off point from where the reader can soar beyond the realms of fancy.

Poetic Justice

The dictionary meaning of the term 'poetic justice' is an outcome in which vice is punished and virtue rewarded, usually in a manner peculiarly or ironically appropriate. Poetic justice is thus somewhat similar to *karma* and can be summed up by the phrases, 'He got what was coming to him', or 'She got what she deserved.' But what is poetic justice in Premchand's *Godan*? Some Shakespearean plays follow it, some do not. Premchand's story *Kafan* discards the limitations of poetic justice that correspond to common expectations from his readers. Premchand was mainly concerned with the injustices of *savarna* classes, but Nishank is one of the next-to-next-generation of writers who is able to see the new social environment taking shape in India. His journalistic background, like Premchand's, is able to make him look through the moral economy of our time. He is able to justify the ways of men to men and see through the veiled harmony of things and events. Look at the following lines:

> 'खून लग गया है इन दीवारों पर' वह महिला कभी रोती तो कभी हँसती। लोग कहते कि वह पागल हो गई है। वह अभागी वृद्धा सुंद्रा थी, जिसने एक बार फिर से अपना बेटा खो दिया था।[8]
>
> ('Blood is smeared on these walls' the woman laughed and wept at times. People said that she had lost her senses. That unfortunate old woman was Sundara, who

had lost the apple of her eye, 'her son', once again.)

The element of poetic justice seems to be missing, but on an average, we find that the novelist in Dr. Nishank wants a happy and prosperous life for his characters. He seldom signs off with a nasty or pessimistic remark. The following line is an example:

> इस सौभाग्य को ईश्वर का प्रसाद समझ सुकन्या ने मन-ही-मन स्वीकार किया और आगे बढ़कर जानकी के चरण छू लिये।[9]
> (Sukanya accepted this good fortune as God's gift. She stepped ahead and touched Janaki's feet.)

Look at the ultimate comment of the novelist when he writes the following, with the end of the novel becoming a place of revelation and understanding:

> पलभर में ही सूर्य अस्त होने वाला था फिर से नवजीवन की उल्लास भरी नवतरंग लिये एक नई सुबह लाने के लिए।[10]
> (The sun was about to set in an instant, to bring a new dawn to the new life's euphoria...)

> थोड़ी ही देर में बस आ गई। गाँव के सभी लोगों का अभिवादन स्वीकार कर पल्लवी बस में बैठ गई और चल पड़ी अपने वास्तविक अभियान की ओर।[10] (पल्लवी, अंतिम पंक्ति)
> (After some time the bus arrived. Receiving farewell greetings from all the villagers, Pallavi sat in the bus and paced towards her real sojourn.)

Don't you think that this might have been a beautiful beginning of this novel and the whole story could be retold in flashback from this point? The use of words 'that woman', 'once again', etc. arouse our curiosity when we look at the end to decide the novel's readability.

Dr. Nishank has been variously described in literary circles as the harbinger of Uttarakhand for his lively and life-like portrayal of the characters of the region. For instance, in the novel *Bira*, the protagonist is a woman, mother-power and a representative character of the region. This is the proper end of a novel in which the beginning of a new dawn shines resplendently.

> "तो ठीक है दीपक! हम जैसे पूर्व में थे, वैसे ही मित्र बने रहेंगे। आज से हमारा संकल्प है कि साथ-साथ चलकर हम इस पिछड़े पहाड़ी क्षेत्र को एक नई दिशा देने का हर संभव प्रयत्न करेंगे। जिन पुनीत कार्यों का तुम अपनी संस्था के साथ संचालन कर रहे हो, उसमें मैं सिर्फ कदम-से-कदम मिलाकर तुम्हारी हर संभव मदद ही नहीं करूँगी, बल्कि एक स्वावलंबी महिला होने के नाते तुम से भी दो कदम आगे बढ़कर इस भगीरथ अभियान में हमेशा आहुति देती रहूँगी। यही होगी हमारे इतने वर्षों के सच्चे स्नेह की परिणति।" बीरा के स्वर में दृढ़ निश्चय था।[11]
>
> ("Then it's okay Deepak! We shall remain friends as we were before. From today onwards it is our resolve that we shall try our level best to provide a new direction to our wretched hilly terrain. You have been managing your welfare institution for the good of the people. I will not only help you in your efforts with all possible means but also fully engage myself in this virtuous endeavour keeping two paces ahead of you. This will mark the culmination of our true affection of so many years." In Bira's voice there was a firm resolution.)

Dr. Nishank, through his writings, has aimed at helping the marginalised who have been suffering injustice but seldom blame their destiny. Premchand, according to Alok Rai, had first to create the 'guilty reader' for his 'literature of conscience' which then helped to disturb the moral economy of his day by attaching a stigma of 'wrong' to behaviour that seemed then unobjectable.[12] Dr. Nishank, on the other hand, doesn't fall in the conventional trap of discourses, such as Dalit and tribal ones, etc. Those, who have been trying to perpetuate the traditional logic of caste system and invoke *Manu-smriti* every time, will find no support here. The idea of 'guilty reader' is reformulated into a 'conscious reader' who is self-aware and self-tutored in the school of universal humanity.

I quoted the first line ('It was the best of times; it was the worst of times'...) of Dickens' novel *A Tale of Two Cities* in the first chapter and now in this last chapter, I use the closing sentence of the same novel, "It is a far, far better thing that I do, than I have ever done; it is a far, far better rest that I go to than I have ever known."[13] The end is thus our beginning of reading the text, which I very sincerely call Dr. Nishank's text. It's not about the destination; it's about the journey.

फिर भी दोष दिखे यदि कोई, हलवे में कंकड़ सा।
क्षमा करें कवि को कोविद जन, वृषारूढ़ शंकर-सा ॥[14]

□

Notes

Chapter 1

1. *Isavasyopanishad, Shukl Yajurveda* (40th chapter), *mantra* 15.
2. Francis Bacon, *Essays* (1597).
3. Friedrich Nietzsche, *On Truth and Lies in an Extra Moral Sense* (1873, p.3).
4. *Deevan-e-Meer* ({Ed.}, Ali Sardar Jafri), (1960, p.23).
5. Emily Dickinson, *The Complete Poems* (1976: poem no. 1263).
6. Salman Rushdie, *Is Nothing Sacred?* (Herbert Read Memorial Lecture, 1990).
7. Derrida, cited in Gopal Sharma (2018: p.350).
8. Ramesh Pokhriyal 'Nishank', *Trust Hard Work Not Destiny* (2012, p. V).
9. Thomas Gray, *Elegy Written in a Country Churchyard.* www.thomasgray.org
10. C.W.F. Hegel ({Ed.} A. Singh & R. Mohapatra) *Reading Hegel: The Introductions* (1991, p.7).
11. Francis Ponge, *The Two-way Text* (1991, p.7).
12. William Blake ({Ed.} Michael Mason) *Selected Poetry* (1998, p. x).
13. Robert Frost, *The Road not Taken* (1920).

14. Geoffrey Bennington. *Interrupting Derrida* (cited by Gopal Sharma, 2018).
15. Normal Holland (1980, p.123-124).
16. T.S. Eliot, *The Sacred Wood* (1920, p. 20).
17. V.S. Naipaul, *An Area of Darkness* (cited in *Mirrorwork: 50 years of Indian Writing*, 1947-1997).
18. Raghuvir Sahay, *Angrezi*. www.hindisamaya.com
19. Premchand, cited in R.B. Sharma (1978, p. 350)
20. Raja Rao, *The Caste of English* (1978, p. 420-422). www.hrm.mhrd.gov.in>ministers-profile

Chapter 2

* Marcel Duchamp, *The Creative Act*, April 1957.

1. *Kabir Granathavali* ({Ed.} Shyam Sundar Das). Guru ko ang.
2. Rabindranath Tagore, *Gitanjali* (1912, poem 35).
3. Namvar Singh, *Kavita aur Rajniti* (2003, p. 216).
4. Ramesh Pokhriyal 'Nishank', *Matrabhumi ke Liye* (2009, p. 15).
5. George Orwell, *Why I Write*. (1946, www.orwell.ru).
6. Joan Didion, *Why I Write* (1976,).
7. *Premchand*, cited in Gopal Sharma (2018, p.241).
8. Nishank, *Tutate Dayare* (2010/2012, p. 13).
9. Nishank, *Meel ke Patthar* (2010, p.13).
10. Nishank, *Pratigya* (2013, p.5).

Chapter 3

1. Andrew Bennett and Nicholas Royal, *An Introduction to Literature Criticism and Theory*, (2016, p.88-89).
2. Nishank, *Nishant* (blurb, 2008, side 2).
3. Nishank, *Nishant* (blurb, 2008, side 3).
4. Yogendra Nath Sharma 'Arun' (Ed.), *Dr Nishank ke Upanyason mein Jeevan Darshan* (2019, p.105).

5. *Edward Said on Contrapuntal Reading*, George M. Wilson (1994, pp.265-273).
6. Nishank, *Nishant* (2008, p.6).
7. Rakesh Batabyal, *JNU: The Making of a University* (2015, p.7).
8. Namvar Singh (Doordarshan, June 23, 2015).
9. *Deccan Herald* (January 6, 2020).
10. Ram Swarup Chaturvedi, *Hindi Sahitya aur Samvedna ke Vikas* (1986, p. 322).
11. Nishank, *Apna Paraya*, (2015, p. 9).
12. Yogendra Nath Sharma 'Arun' (Ed.), *Dr. Nishank ke Upanyason mein Jeevan Darshan* (Bhumika, 2019, p. 5).
13. Bachchan, *Nisha Nimantran* (Bhumika, 1938, p. 17).
14. Normal Holland, *'Unity Identity Text Itself' in Reader-Response Criticism* (1980, 123-124).
15. Yogendra Nath Sharma 'Arun' (Ed.), *Dr. Nishank ke Upanyason mein Jeevan Darshan*, (2019, p. 101).
16. Ibid, Harishankar Mishra (2019, p. 74).
17. Nishank, *Ai Vatan Tere Liye* (2006, p. xv).
18. Radha Kamal Mukherjee, *The Social Structure of Values* (1950, p. 56).
19. Brandon Sanderson, *Creative Writing Class Lectures* (April 14, 2012).

Chapter 4

1. T.S. Eliot, *Tradition and the Individual Talent*, www.tseliot.com
2. Agyeya, (*Bhavanti*, 1996, p. 11).
3. http://classics.mit.edu/plato/republic
4. Suvir Kaul, *Poems of a Nation: Anthems of Empire* (2009, p. 8).
5. Philippe Lacoue-Labarthe (1999, p. 21).
6. Wallace Stevens, *Materia Poetica.*

7. Emily Dickinson to Thomas Higginson. www.theatlantic.com>archive>
8. Edward C. Dimock, *The Literatures of India* (1975).
9. Allama Iqbal, *Himala*, 1905. www.rekhta.com
10. Ramdhari Singh 'Dinkar', *Himalaya*, www.kavitakosh.org
11. Babu Syam Sundar Das cited by Dalmiya (1997, p. 32).
12. Ram Swarup Chaturvedi, *Hindi Sahitya aur Samvedna ka Vikas*, (1986, p. 46).
13. R.S. MacGegor, *Hindi Literature of the Nineteenth and Early Twentieth Centuries* (1974, p. 109).
14. Lothar Lutze, *Sahitya Vividh Sandarbh* (1968, p. 83).
15. Akshaya Kumar, *Poetry, Politics and Culture* (2009, p. 38).
16. Yogendra Nath Sharma 'Arun' (Ed.), *Dr. Nishank ke Kavya mein Indradhanushi Chintan* (2019, p. 5).
17. A.K. Ramanujan, *Any Cow's Horn can Do It* (1995, p. 94).
18. Nishank, *Jeevan Path Mein*, Dr. Harimohan's preface (2009, p. 7).
19. Nishank, *Andhera Ja Raha Hai* (2017, p. 28).
20. *Swayam Ko Jana hai Maine* (2008, p. 13).
21. Nishank, *Sangharsh Jari Hai*, (2009, p.74).
22. P.B. Shelley, *To a Skylark*. www.poetryfoundation.org
23. Jai Shankar Prasad, *Ansu. www.hindi_kavita.com*
24. Nishank, *Prateeksha*, (2005/2015, Kranti Parv, 1).
25. Nishank, *Prateeksha* (2005/2015, Aradhna, xvi).
26. Robert Frost, *Waiting*.
27. Nishank, *Prateeksha* (2005/2015, p. xvi).
28. Nishank, *Din bhar Nithalle Rrahkar*.
29. Madan Mohan Malaviya cited in Francesca Orsini, *The Hindi Public Sphere: Language, Literature and the Politics of Nationalism* (2009).
30. *The Indian Express*, 13 June,2017.
31. Ibid.

32. Atal Bihari Vajpayee, *Meri Ikkyavan Kavitayen* (2006, p. 123).
33. *Frontline* (October 23, 2004).
34. Nishank, *Yugpurush Bharatratna Atalji* (2016, p. 8).
35. *The Print* (7 June, 2019).
36. Nishank, *Srijan ke Beej* (2020, p. 47).
37. Nishank, *Sangharsh Jari Hai* (2009,).
38. Nishank, *Bhul Pata Nahin* (2019, p. 1).
39. Ibid (p. 65).
40. Nishank, *Bhul Pata Nahin* (2019, p. 8).
41. Nishank, *Desh Hhum Jalne an Denge* (2009, p. 15-16).
42. Nishank, *Mujhe Vidhata Banna Hhai* (2005, p. 20).
43. Agyeya (1989, p. 29).
44. *Derrida*, cited in Gopal Sharma (2018, p. 27).
45. Robert Frost. *Conversations on the Crafts of Poetry*.
46. Francis Pongee
47. Chetana Pokhriyal (Trans.), *The Darkness is Vanishing* (2019, p. 5-6).
48. Ibid. (2019, p. 30).
49. Benedict Anderson, *Imagined Communities* (1991, p. 6).
50. Chetna Pokhriyal, *The Seeds of Creation* (2019, p.5-9)
51. George Steiner, *After Babel* (1976, p. 298).

Chapter 5

1. Ngugi wa Thiong'o, *Decolonising the Mind* (1992, p. 11).
2. Quoted in *ThePenguin Gandhi Reader* (Ed.) Rudrangshu Mukherjee (1993, p. 26).
3. *Ananda Kentish Coomaraswamy*, cited by Gopal Sharma (2018, p. 197).
4. Nishank, *Bhul Pata Nahin* (2019, p. 9).
5. Nishank, *Samarpan* (2005, p. 11).
6. Atal Bihari Vajpayee, used in 'Nishank'on blurb side 2 (*Nishant*, 2008).

7. Seamus Heaney, *Nobel Lectures* (1995).
8. Nishank, *Mere Sankalp* (2008, p. 55).
9. Nishank, *Mere Sankalp* (2008, p. 31).
10. Ruskin Bond, *The Room on the Roof* (2016, p. 25).
11. Nishank, *Vivekananda in the Himalayas* (2018, p. IX).
12. Nishank, *Selected Stories of Dr. Ramesh Pokhriyal 'Nishank'*, (2017, preface).
13. Nishank, *Ei Watan Tere Liye* (2006, p. XIII).
14. Nishank, *Selected Stories of Dr. Ramesh Pokhriyal 'Nishank'* (2017, preface).

Chapter 6

1. Cited by Harold Bloom, *Stendhal: Comprehensive Research and Study Guide* (2009).
2. Nishank, *Pratigya* (2013, p. 7).
3. Susan Sontag (2007, p. 215).
4. William Shakespeare, *Richard II* (3.2).
5. Nishank, *Major Nirala* (p. 90-91).
6. Nishank, *Apna Paraya* (2015, p.25).
7. Nishank, Pallavi (2005, p. 9).
8. Shivpoojan Sahay, *Kahani ka Plot*. www.hindisamay.com
9. Rajendra Yadav, *Aadmi ki Nigah mein Aurat* (2001, p. 5).
10. Nishank, *Chut Gaya Padav* (2010, p. 17).
11. Nishank, *Pralay ke Beech* (2018, p. 25).

Chapter 7

1. Nishank, *Selected Stories* (preface).
2. Upendranath *'Ashk', Girti Diwaren* (Falling Walls) translated by Rockwell (2015, Introduction).
3. Nishank, *Meel ke Patthar* (2010, p. 13).
4. Nishank, *Tutate Dayre* (2010/2012, p. 56).
5. Nishank, *Disaster of Kedarnath* (2018, p. 27.)
6. Ibid. (p. 57).

7. Nishank, *Selected Stories of Ramesh Pokhriyal 'Nishank'* (2017, p. 6).
8. Ibid. (p. 35).
9. Nishank, *Mere Sankalp, Theeya* (2008, p. 26).
10. Nishank, *Ek Kahani* or, *Garibi Hatao* (2008, p. 5).
11. Nishank, *Naya Gyanodaya* (February 2014).
12. Nishank, *Antheen* (*Ek Thi Juhi*) (2014/2016, p.130).
13. Nishank, *Tutate Dayaare* (2010/2012, p. 13).

Chapter 8

* K. Balasubramania Iyer, *Yaksha Prashna* (1989, *shloka* 114).

1. Nishank, *Trust Hard Work Not Destiny* (2012, P.5).
2. Nishank, *Inspiration for the World* (2019, p. III).
3. Nishank, *Swami Vivekanand* (2012, P. X).
4. Nishank, *Dreams that don't Let You Sleep* (2016, p. 16).
5. Ibid. (p. 111).
6. Nishank, *Inspiration for the World* (p. VI).
7. Yogendra Nath Sharma 'Arun', *Kathakar Nishank ke Upanyason mein Jeevan Mulya* (2017, p. 5).
8. Ibid. (p. 8).
9. Ibid. (p. 12).

Chapter 9

1. *Derrida* cited by Gopal Sharma (2018, p. 36).
2. Frank Kermode (1967, p. 8).
3. Nishank, *Nishant* (2008, p. 5).
4. Ibid. (2008, p. 103).
5. Nishank, *Mere Sankalp, Theeya* (2008, p. 26).
6. Nishank, *Antheen* (2016, p. 75).
7. Nishank, *Apna Paraya* (2015, p. 159).
8. Nishank, *Pratigya* (2013, p. 152).
9. Nishank, *Krataghn* (2015, p. 152).

10. Nishank, *Beera* (2008, p. 17).
11. Nishank, *Beera*, (2008, p. 170).
12. Alok Rai cited in *Justice, Political, Judicial* (Ed.) Rajiv Bhargava and others (2008, p. 37).
13. Charles Dickens, *A Tale of Two Cities* (1859, p. 320).
14. Nishank, *Pratiksha* (2015, p. XVI).

□

List of Published Books

Books written by Dr. Ramesh Pokhriyal 'Nishank'

(Updated and received as on 31 May, 2020)

Selection of Short Stories

1. *Roshni ki Eik Kiran,* Sahitya Niketan, Bijnore
2. *Bas Eik hi Ichcha,* Sahitya Niketan, Bijnore
3. *Kya Nahin ho Sakta,* Sahitya Niketan, Bijnore
4. *Bheed Sakshi Hai*, Sahitya Niketan, Bijnore
5. *Aik aur Kahani,* Vani Prakashan, Delhi
6. *Mere Sankalp,* Vani Pprakashan, Delhi
7. *Vipada Jeevit Hai,* Winsar Publishing, Dehradun
8. *Khade Hue Prashn,* Winsar Publishing, Dehradun
9. *Tutate Daayre,* Vani Prakashan, Delhi
10. *Meel ke Patthar,* Vani Prakashan, Delhi
11. *Aao Seekhen Kahaniyon Se,* Diamond Books, Delhi
12. *Antheen,* Rajkamal Prakashan, Delhi
13. *Vah Jindagi,* Prabhat Prakashan, Delhi
14. *Kedarnath Aapda Ki Sachchi Kahaniyan,* Prabhat Prakashan, Delhi
15. *Kathayen Pahadon Ki*, Prabhat Prakashan, Delhi
16. *Nishank kee Sarvsreshth Ikkis Kahaniya,* Diamond Books, Delhi

Selections of Poetry

17. *Samarpan,* Prabhat Prakashan, Delhi
18. *Navankur,* Prabhat Prakashan, Delhi
19. *Mujhe Vidhata Banna Hai,* Prabhat Prakashan, Delhi
20. *Tum bhi Mere Saath Chalo,* Sahitya Niketan, Bijnore
21. *Desh Ham Jalne na Denge,* Sahitya Niketan, Bijnore
22. *Jeevan Path Mein,* Sahitya Niketan, Bijnore
23. *Matrbhumi ke Liye,* Sahitya Niketan, Bijnore
24. *Sangharsh Jari Hai,* Sahitya Niketan, Bijnore
25. *Koi Mushkil Nahin,* Winsar Publishing Company, Dehradun
26. *Ei Watan Tere Liye,* Winsar Publishing Company, Dehradun
27. *Andhera Ja Raha Hai,* Prabhat Prakashan, Delhi
28. *Srijan ke Beej,* Prabhat Prakashan, Delhi
29. *Bhul Pata Nahin,* Vani Prakashan, Delhi
30. *Pratiksha* (*Khand Kavya*), Winsar Publishing, Dehradun

Novels

31. *Major Nirala,* Vani Prakashan, Delhi
32. *Pahad se Uncha,* Vani Prakashan, Delhi
33. *Beera,* Vani Prakashan, Delhi
34. *Nishant,* Bhavana Prakashan, Delhi
35. *Chuut Gaya Padav,* Vani Prakashan, Delhi
36. *Apna Paraya*
37. *Pallavi,* Bharatiya Jnanpith, Delhi
38. *Pratigya,* Prabhat Prakashan, Delhi
39. *Kritaghn,* Prabhat Prakashan, Delhi
40. *Bhagonvali,* Prabhat Prakashan, Delhi
41. *Shikhron ke Sangharsh,* Vani Prakashan, Delhi

Tourism, Religion and Culture

42. *Dharti ka Swarg* (one), Winsar Publishing, Dehradun
43. *Dharti ka Swarg* (two), Winsar Publishing, Dehradun
44. *Dharti ka Swarg* (three), Winsar Publishing, Dehradun
45. *Bharatiya Sanskriti, Sabhyata evam Parampara*, Diamond Books, Delhi

Personality Development

46. *Safalta ke Achuk Mantra,* Diamond Books, Delhi
47. *Karm par Vishvas Karen, Bhagya par Nahin,* Diamond Books, Delhi
48. *Sansar Kayaron ke Liye Nahin,* Rajkamal Prakashan, Delhi
49. *Sapne Jo Sone na Dein*, Diamond Books, Delhi

Diary/Memoirs/Travelogues

50. *Pralay ke Beech*, Diomond Books, Delhi
51. *Mauritus kee Swarnim Smritiyan,* Prabhat Prakashan, Delhi
52. *Nepal mein Eik Din*, Prabhat Prakashan, Delhi
53. *Khushiyon ka Desh, Bhutan*, Prabhat Prakashan, Delhi
54. *Bharatiya Sanskriti ka Samvahak*, Prabhat Prakashan, Delhi

Children's Literature

55. *Karmayogi Vivekananda* (Hindi/English), Diamond Books, Delhi
56. *Sakaratmak Soch Swami Vivekananda* (Hindi, English), Diamond Books, Delhi
57. *Chicago mein Swami Vivekananda* (Hindi/English), Diamond Bbooks, Delhi

58. *Aage Badho Swami Vivekananda* (Hindi, English), Diomond Books, Delhi
59. *Aao Seekhen Kahaniyon Se*, Diamond Books, Delhi

Edited Books

60. *Mere Patr Meri Katha*

Translations in Different Indian Languages

1. *Khade hue Prashn, En Kelvikku Ennabathil*, Tamil
2. *Ei Vatan Tere Liye, Tayanade Unakkad*, Tamil
3. *Ei Vatan Tere Liye, Janmabhumi*, Telugu
4. *Sangharsh Jari Hai, Sagutunna Samram*, Telugu
5. *Tutate Daayre, Andhkaram Pai Sammetta Devva*, Telugu
6. *Pratigya, Pratigya*, Telugu
7. *Meel ka Patthar, Melache Dagad*, Marathi
8. *Meel ka Patthar, Melugallugal*, Kannada
9. *Khade Hue Prashn, Prashnankit*, Marathi
10. *Kya Nahin Ho Sakta*, Sanle Shakya Aaahe, Marathi
11. *Sansar Kayron ke Liye Nahin, Personality Development*, Kannada
12. *Bas Eik hi Ichcha, Kathga Louri Hour*, Garhwali
13. *Bas Eik hi Ichcha, Ev Evabhilash*, Sanskrit
14. *Himalaya ka Mahakumbh: Nanda Rajjat, Himalayeey Kumbhah Nanda Rajjatam*, Sanskrit
15. *Safalta ke Achuk Mantra, Personality Development*, in 8 languages
16. *Sapne Jo Sone na Dein, Personality Development*, in 8 languages
17. *Bhagya par Nahin Parishram par Vishvas Karen, Personalty Development*, in 8 languages

Translations in Foreign Languages

1. *Dr. Nishank ki Shreshth Kahaniyan, Selected Stories of Dr. Nishank*, English
2. *Bheed Sakshi Hai, The Crowd Bears Witness*, English
3. *Khade hue Prashn, Esperances Et Verites*, French
4. *Bas Eik hi Ichcha, Nur Ein Wunsch*, German
5. *Khade Hue Prashn*, Du Und Icch, German
6. *Himalaya ka Mahakumbh Nanda Devi Rajjat, Himalaya mahakumbh nanda devi rajjat*, Nepali
7. *Pralaya ke Beech, Pralay Majh Kekarnaath Aapda*, Nepali
8. *Khade Hue Prashn, All but Fiction*, English
9. *Srijan ke Beej, The Seeds of Creation*, English
10. *Andhera Ja Raha Hai, The Darkness is Vanishing*, English

□□□